CHRISTMAS CORPSE AT CARIBOU CABIN

A Lainey Maynard Mystery Book 4

LAURA HERN

CONTENTS

MANY THANKS

Thank you for supporting authors by buying, reading, and reviewing our books. I give you my utmost gratitude! I couldn't continue to tell stories if it weren't for you and for the support team that surrounds me!

SOCIAL MEDIA

Laura Hern Social
Website & Newsletter:
https://www.laurahern.com

Facebook:
https://www.facebook.com/laurahernauthor

Also in series:
The Family Tree Murders
Murder In The Backwater
Curtain Call At Brooksey's Playhouse

And more coming soon!

REVIEWS

"Engaging characters...fun and interesting...enjoyable and light reading...you won't want to put it down!" Janice

"This is a great series. It is light, full of interesting characters and a deep dark mystery! It made me laugh. It made me want to keep reading. I can't wait for the next one. The Whoopee Club is quite the mystery solving team!" Carla

"It's a masterpiece! Fraud investigator Lainey Maynard is told to see one of their insurance customers. The man wants them to investigate the supposed murder of his wife. The mystery has many surprising twists and turns. Highly recommended!" Jerri

CHAPTER 1

The town of Mirror Falls had slipped into its annual pre-winter funk with the end of Daylight Savings Time and the inevitable long days of icy darkness that loomed ahead. Lainey was not looking forward to the dreary weeks with little to no sunshine. The thought of several feet of snow that would soon grace her yard and freeze into blackish piles as the winter progressed was a reminder for her to buy a new snow shovel.

The year had been the busiest and most stressful one that Lainey could remember. The insurance company that employed her had been sold and the new owners increased her workload by at least half. Thanksgiving was a couple of days away and she had already put over 40,000 miles on her KIA, traveling to ten states for difficult fraud investigations. She was tired and looking for some downtime during the upcoming Christmas holiday.

Thankfully, the Whoopee group was meeting tonight for their Thanksgiving dinner and card games. Lainey was bringing her special cauliflower crusted veggie pizza and a Greek salad with her favorite roasted Mediterranean olives. She looked forward to sharing good food and forgetting about work for a short while. The group always met at 5:30 in the evening and took turns hosting. Tonight was Vera's turn.

As Lainey drove onto Vera's street, she noticed Shep's car parked in the driveway.

Hmm, Shep must be joining us. Sure hope he made that razzle-dazzle berry cobbler I love so much! Lainey thought to herself.

She parked her car on the street, got out and carried her dinner contributions to the front door. Before she could ring the doorbell, Francy opened the glass front door and welcomed her in with a huge smile.

"Yea! Lainey's here and she's brought the pizza!"

"Whoop, Whoop!" Della said as she walked from the kitchen to greet Lainey at the door. "I've been hungry for pizza all day. Come inside. I'll take your food to the table."

"Thanks, Della."

Lainey handed her the two containers of food and

quickly took off her shoes and hung her coat in the small entryway closet. The townhome was an open concept design. Her front door opened to a large room that served as the living room, a small dining area, and the kitchen. The vaulted ceiling made the space seem much larger. Vera decorated for every season. Norwegian snowmen gnomes for January. Hearts and redbirds for Valentine's Day. Leprechauns and shamrocks for St. Patrick's Day. If it was a holiday, she had special decor to celebrate it.

Tonight was to celebrate Thanksgiving and Lainey expected to see the usual turkeys, horns of plenty, and pilgrim decorations. Instead, she saw black carved bear figurines and reindeer of all sizes placed around. Pillows on the living room couch were stitched with Welcome to the Cabin and Cabin Living is the Life.

As Lainey walked toward the kitchen, her skin tingled. She felt a familiar feeling of anxiousness in her stomach that forced her intuition into high gear. She'd felt this many times before and it always served as a warning that something unexpected was about to occur.

What in the world? Get a grip! She told herself silently. *This is just the Whoopee group, for Pete's sake. Vera decorated differently this year. What's the big deal?*

"Hurry up, Lainey. We're hungry and we don't want the food to get cold," Shep said as he pulled out a dining room chair for Vera.

"I'm coming, I'm coming." Goosebumps covered her from head to toe and she knew her instincts were on point once again. She sat down across the table from Vera, not knowing that her holiday plans of rest and relaxation were about to change.

CHAPTER 2

Vera Abernathy loved to entertain and had been doing so for almost half a century. She hosted the weekly coffee hour at the Mirror Falls Senior Center every Tuesday morning and brought treats and games to the YMCA's monthly Brunch with a Senior event. She was head of her church's funeral food committee and regularly took treats to the police station where Francy worked. Since she had been dating Shep Morton, the chef and owner of the Backwater Restaurant, she had recruited him to make the goodies she shared. It left her more time to decorate!

Tonight was no exception. A lush hunter green cloth covered the pedestal dining table and the dark color highlighted the crystal wine glasses that sat like royalty in front of each place setting. Vera hadn't used

her Christmas Dickens' dishes, though. In their place
were blue, speckled metal dinner plates and cups.
There was a smorgasbord of food waiting to be
devoured. Pickled beets, tater tot hot dish, veggie pizza,
salad, pinto beans, and barbecued spare ribs filled the
table.

"My goodness, Vera," Della smiled as she gazed at
the steaming variety of food. "I think you've got
everyone's favorite here tonight."

"Shep and I tried to do just that. He was kind
enough to prepare the ribs and..."

"Kind enough? You, my dear, ordered me to make
ribs for Francy and the tater tot hot dish for Della!" He
raised his hand in a mock salute, then leaned toward
her, putting his arm around her shoulders.

"Now, Shep, you just stop that. I did not order you,"
her tone was matter-of-fact, but lightened when he
kissed her cheek. "Well, maybe I encouraged you a little
bit."

Everyone chuckled. What followed were thirty
minutes of laughing, eating, clinking of forks and
knives scraping up delicious bites of food on the metal
plates, and toasts to the hostess.

"I'm completely stuffed!" Lainey grunted, leaning
back in her chair. "I don't think I could hold another
bite."

Shep smiled, scooted his chair back and stood up.
"That's too bad. I guess my razzle-dazzle berry cobbler

with mocha ice cream will have to go into the trash bin."

"Don't you dare throw out one spoonful! I'll make room, even if it kills me!"

He laughed and turned to Vera. "Sweetie, would you help me dish up the dessert?"

"You know I have special bowls for the cobbler." She followed him into the kitchen.

Della, Francy, and Lainey looked at each other and spoke at the same time.

"What's going on with your Mom?" Lainey asked quietly.

"And what's with the chuck wagon dishes and wild animals everywhere?" Della added.

Francy shrugged her shoulders. "You know as much as I do. I've never seen these metal plates or decorations before. Who knows what these two are planning."

"Humph," Vera cleared her throat as she walked back to the table. She spoke like a mother scolding her child. "And what do you mean 'these two are planning', young lady?"

"Mom, I know you. You decorate with a theme in mind. And this is definitely not your favorite pilgrims on the Mayflower decorations."

"Shep and I have a little surprise for you ladies and it starts with dessert!" She handed a sealed envelope to each of them. "Don't open it until I tell you to."

Confusion and skepticism was apparent on the faces of the three friends. Della took hers and sniffed it, checking to see if it had perfume or a scent that might give an idea of what was inside. But there was nothing.

"Here's your winter wonderland vacation dessert, ladies. Enjoy!" Shep said proudly as he presented the cobbler and ice cream.

Each serving was in a large white coffee mug. Around the top and bottom of each mug was a red plaid band. The words 'Welcome to Reindeer Lodge' were across the top band and the the words 'Hot Cocoa, Sleigh Rides, Fun' were written in the bottom band. The middle of the cup resembled an old, grayish wooden fence. A reindeer with large antlers stood in front of it.

"Wait a second," Francy began, "I've heard of Reindeer Lodge, but I can't remember why."

"Your dad and I spent our honeymoon there," Vera smiled. "Open your envelopes!"

Giggles, oohs, and ahs followed as the contents of the envelopes were revealed. Inside each was a photo of a very young Vera and Doc Abernathy hugging each other in front of the lodge. Also inside was a coupon for a free hot cocoa and a folded handwritten note which read 'You have my utmost thanks.' It was signed by Jim McAndrews.

"I love the photo, but who is Jim and why is he thanking us?" Lainey asked. Della and Francy nodded.

"Paul and I have friends who have gone to Reindeer Lodge for years for their family reunion," Della stated. "But since the pandemic hit a couple of years ago, they haven't been back. I didn't think it was still open."

"You've hit the nail on the head, Della," Vera answered. "Shep can fill you in better than I can."

"Eat your cobbler while it's still hot and I'll tell you the entire story," he said.

The ladies ate and Shep began explaining. He and Jim McAndrews served together in the 3rd Battalion, 325th Airborne Infantry at Fort Bragg, North Carolina.

"The 3rd of the 325th was assigned to the 82nd Airborne Division. Jim and I met during combat night jumps in1973 and have remained friends since," Shep smiled. "He always thought his parachute wasn't going to open."

Everyone had finished their dessert and were listening intently to his story.

"Tell them how Jim married after the service, bought the Reindeer Lodge and has been running it all these years," Vera urged. "They want to hear about the vaca…"

"Mom, let him finish!" Francy rolled her eyes and sighed.

"She tells me to get to the point all the time," he took hold of Vera's hand and continued. "She's correct. Jim and his wife ran the lodge quite successfully. They had two boys and had made plans to retire one day, hoping one son would take it over."

He paused for a moment and his voice cracked when he spoke again. "But life doesn't go the way we plan. Vera and I have experienced that. Jim's wife died six years ago and since then, he's done the best he could."

The ladies listened while Shep explained that for the last three years, Jim had been struggling to make ends meet. He finally realized that his only option was to sell the lodge after the current Christmas season.

There was a subtle feeling of sadness as the five people sat silently, thinking about Jim and the lodge.

"What about his sons?" Lainey asked. "Would one of them buy it or run it?"

"I'm not sure of the details, but the older son is a financial advisor and has no desire to be involved with the lodge. The younger son works as his dad's general handyman-maintenance guy," Shep answered.

"Jim is the chef and has been doing the housekeeping duties since his wife passed," Vera shook her head. "It's my understanding that Kevin, the younger son, isn't a chef or interested in being a chef. It seems he doesn't have the finances to buy it either."

Della stood up and began clearing the table. "Okay. Francy and Lainey and I will clear the table so we can play cards. Shep, you and Vera stay seated and tell us why Jim is thanking us."

"Great idea," Francy said. "You two take turns or Mom, let Shep speak. Either way, spill the rest of the story!"

"Well, I see that the bossy gene definitely runs in the family!" Shep grinned.

"She does take after me, doesn't she?" Vera chided proudly. "That's the Abernathy women for you!"

The sadness in the air evaporated and the room filled with laughter once more.

"Last week, Jim called me...from the hospital. He was involved in a snowmobile accident," Shep said. "He suffered a broken arm, damaged rotator cuff, and a broken leg."

"He wants Shep to come to the lodge to cook and keep it running through the Christmas holidays," Vera chimed in. "And I'm going with him!"

"We want all of you to go with us," Shep added.

The ladies looked at each other in disbelief. Francy was the first to speak.

"A free Christmas vacation at a lodge in northern Minnesota? I'm in!"

"Count me in, too!" Della replied.

"That's just what I have been needing. A vacation with Shep's food and hot cocoa!" Lainey exclaimed. "I'd go today if I could."

Shep and Vera looked at each other hesitantly.

"We'd like you to drive up with us the day after Thanksgiving," Vera said sheepishly.

The goosebumps Lainey first felt had gone away once she sat down to eat. But now, they were back and she felt a little nauseous.

"Wait a second, what else are you not telling us?" she questioned. "There's more to this, isn't there."

It was Vera who rolled her eyes this time.

"Shep and I drove to the Rainy Lake Medical Center in International Falls to see Jim last weekend. His son Kevin was there and he took us to the lodge after our visit."

"The lodge needs work and..." Shep paused. "It needs a very thorough cleaning."

"I've never seen so many dust bunnies in corners in my life!" Vera frowned and shivered. "I despise those darn things!"

Della crossed her arms and looked at Francy. One side of Francy's mouth was turned up in a snarl. Lainey nodded her head slowly.

"And that is why the cabin-looking decorations and our favorite dishes tonight. Bribery at its best!" she winked at Shep.

"Let me get this straight," Della began. "A free vacation – if we become the Whoopee Merry Maids Cleaning Service, correct?"

"Well..." Vera started to speak.

"Don't try to deny it, Mom," Francy kidded.

Shep gave a big belly laugh. "Yep! It was all Vera's idea!"

"Why you old goat!" She pretended to be offended, but then grinned. "The cleaning crew *was* my idea, but *you* bought the mugs!"

"Okay, okay," Lainey laughed. "Is there internet service at the Lodge? I do have vacation time, but I will need to do some work if we are planning on staying a couple of weeks."

Once again Vera looked at Shep and shrugged her shoulders. "You wanna answer that?"

"Yes, but both cell and internet service can be spotty. If you have work or need better service, Ranier or International Falls are only a few miles away. I'm sure either town will have a coffee shop or two." He paused to gage their reactions before continuing carefully.

"Actually, we need you to stay until after Christmas. Della could bring Paul and Francy could bring Roger. Wouldn't that..."

"Hold on," Francy interrupted, raising her hand. "Stay for a month? Bring Roger and Paul?" She crossed her arms and leaned back her chair.

"Something sounds very fishy to me," Della replied, leaning forward, clasping her hands together, placing them on the table in front or her. "In fact, it smells as bad as Shep's stink bait concoction."

"I hear ice fishing is great up there," Vera chimed in with a forced chuckle, hoping to smooth over the questions she knew were coming next.

Lainey sat quietly, listening and watching Shep and Vera's body language. She took in a deep breath and blew it out, shaking her head as if to wake herself up. Then she spoke.

"It seems we're to be the housekeeping staff for the holidays," pointing her finger at the two sitting across from her. "You two think you're pretty sneaky, don't you?"

"I know it's a lot to ask," Shep began as his voiced cracked once more. "It's just that Jim's finances are gone and selling this lodge is his last resort to avoid bankruptcy or foreclosure. We…" his eyes teared up and he had to stop for a moment before going on. "We are his only hope."

Della, Francy, and Lainey glanced at each other and without hesitation agreed.

"Thank you, girls," Shep replied.

"Your smile is enough thanks for us," Della said.

"Now do you girls see why I let this old goat be my boyfriend? He has a heart of gold!" Vera announced proudly.

"And he's a great cook, too!" Francy teased.

"Well, there is that," Vera grinned.

"Enough of the flattery…you're making this old man blush! I'll make sure you are all fed very well! Now, are we going to play cards or not?" Shep laughed.

CHAPTER 3

The rest of the evening was spent playing dominoes, Yahtzee, and gin rummy. Talk revolved around the upcoming trip to Reindeer Lodge and the fact that there were only three days to prepare. It was decided that Shep and Vera would drive up in one car, and Lainey, Della, and Francy in another.

"Let's meet tomorrow at Babe's House of Caffeine and figure out the details," Francy said. "Lainey, are you on the road for work tomorrow?"

"I'm in town but have Zoom meetings in the morning. How about meeting for a quick lunch?"

The ladies agreed and Francy said she would arrive early and get their favorite table.

"Well, I can tell you right now that Paul cannot go

to the Lodge," Della stated. "The holidays can be very busy for morticians. No way could he be gone for several weeks."

"And I can speak for Roger. It would bore him to death staying there for a month," Francy mused. "So, it will be the three of us."

"Sorry to break this up, but it's getting late and I need to be going," Shep apologized. "Craig and Cindy Poe are going to take care of the Backwater Restaurant while I'm gone and we have a meeting bright an early tomorrow morning."

He gathered his coat and Vera walked him to the door. He leaned in to give her a kiss and she backed up slightly. She looked over her shoulder and nodded her head toward the kitchen.

"Not in front of the girls," she whispered loudly enough that everyone in the room heard.

He looked at the ladies sitting around the table, waved at them, and winked. Then he took Vera into his arms, and planted a long, lingering kiss smack dab on her lips. He stepped back, and grinning ear to ear, he bowed. But before walking out the door, he turned to the ladies and said, "Take that, Cary Grant!"

Vera's face was flushed and she looked as if stars were shooting out of her eyes. She quickly gathered her emotions and turned to the others.

"And he calls *me* bossy!"

Everyone laughed as they gathered their dishes and headed to their cars to drive home.

The next morning, Lainey was up early checking her email and calendar. On a normal workday, she received sixty-five to eighty emails, all stating they needed her immediate attention. Over her years as a fraud investigator, she had become very good at prioritizing tasks.

"If I won't have a strong internet connection, I better see if I can reschedule a few things," she said aloud as she waited for the computer system to boot up.

Lainey walked into the kitchen to brew her morning fix of java. Her coffee maker had died, worn out from years of heating water and spitting out whatever her current flavor of coffee was that day. She had been waiting for Black Friday deals to order a new one. In the meantime, she had an electric water kettle and a pour over coffee strainer. She was making a cup of coffee when she heard her office phone ringing.

She hurried back to her computer screen and clicked to answer the incoming call.

"Good morning. This is Lainey."

A familiar voice answered her. It was Clyde Bedlow, fondly referred to as Snoops among her fellow investigators. During the time she worked at the corporate headquarters in Houston, Texas, his office was just down the hall from hers. When she was a newbie agent, naïve and inexperienced, he had taken her under his wing and taught her more than she could ever thank him for.

"It's been a long time since I've heard from you," he said cordially. "How's Minnesota treating you?"

"Snoops! It's good to hear from you! I've missed your grumpy voice asking me to bring you coffee every morning. Did I read somewhere that you were retiring?"

"Retire? Me? You've been in the frozen tundra too long! What would this office do without me?" he chuckled.

"Close down is my guess!" she giggled.

"When the new owners took over, they assigned me to a unique position. I remained the head of our cyber/computer department and was given the task of vetting new complaints or cases that were filed. And as of last week, I began assigning verified cases to agents."

"Congratulations! And I thought you were busy before. When do you find time to sleep?"

"Before you get carried away, listen a minute."

His voice changed instantly from the friendly mentor to the serious tone she had heard many times over the years. She knew he meant business.

"Yes, sir. I'm listening."

"We've been retained to investigate an

embezzlement situation," he began. "It appears to have been occurring over several years and affects many clients. The business is located in your neck of the woods."

"I've handled these type of cases before. If the owner has documented proof, it might be an open and shut case. Is the business in the Twin Cities area?"

"There are a couple of twists with this one, Lainey."

"What twists?"

"Blackmail and…" he hesitated. "Possibly murder."

"Murder?" she blurted out.

"Possibly. You are one of our most experienced investigators. However, I am concerned that this could be a very dangerous situation."

"Snoops, you know I do not back away from any case."

"That's exactly why I am concerned."

There was an awkward silence. She did not respond immediately, weighing carefully what her next words should be.

"I have relationships with several law enforcement departments and officials throughout Minnesota. I have worked cases where they called me in and where I had to call them in."

"Yes, I have reviewed all the cases you've handled since moving to Mirror Falls. You are thorough and detailed, just like I taught you to be."

"You were an excellent teacher." She remembered how difficult it was to please him when she was training. How many reports she had retyped because she left out a date or had an incorrect fact. How many times had she walked confidently into his office with a completed practice scenario file, only to have him tell her she missed the main points and to start again. It seemed like thousands.

"Flattery won't change my concern. I'm torn whether to assign this to you or fly someone from the office to work it."

Lainey felt the hair on the back of her neck stand and the muscles in her jaw tense up. The last time the company flew someone in from the home office, he drank himself into a stupor the first night he was in town. He tried to drive back to his hotel, got pulled over, and spent the night in jail for DUI. She had to bail him out the next morning. He was sick for two days.

Take a breath, Lainey. The last thing he needs to hear in your voice is anger.

She took a couple of breaths and did her best to relax her jaw before she responded.

"If you tell me the details of the case, perhaps we can decide whether I'm the right agent."

She knew her response sounded forced…because it was. And Snoops knew it, too.

"Agreed. Let me give you the basics of the case," he

replied. "Then, if I decide you are getting the case, I'll email you the details."

Over the next few minutes, Snoops explained they had received a call from a woman claiming to be the wife of an employee in an investment company in northern Minnesota. They had accused her husband of embezzling hundreds of thousands of dollars from clients. When he tried to explain he was being setup and was innocent, his boss fired him and threatened to prosecute. She found him dead the next day in their apartment. The police said it was a self-inflicted gunshot wound, but the wife says he was murdered and she has proof he was innocent.

"Is this a fraud investigation or a wrongful death case?" Lainey asked.

"That is what you need to find out...and why I said it could be a very dangerous investigation."

He coughed and cleared his throat. She could hear him pick up a glass and take a drink of something, probably cold coffee.

Here goes. Be brave...be bold...be careful what you promise him.

"I know I can handle this case, Snoops. And if it looks like it might be a murder investigation, I will contact law enforcement as soon as possible. Does that put your mind at ease?"

The silence on the other end of the phone was deafening and the longer it lasted, the more anxious she felt. Finally, he cleared his throat once more and answered her.

"Not at ease, but I will assign you to the case."

"Thank you. Send me the information and I'll get to work on it."

"Remember this. I will keep tabs on this investigation…and on you," he warned.

"Yes, sir. I will remember that."

"Good. I'll email you the files that I have later this morning. Let me know when you receive them."

"Sure thing. And thank you for trusting me with this."

"You may not thank me when I tell you the wife wants to meet with you as soon as possible. I know you were hoping to take some time off, but you're going to be working on this immediately and it could last through December." He expected to hear her complain a bit. But he heard nothing.

"Where in the Twin Cities does she live?" She asked.

"It's not the Twin Cities area. The town is International Falls and it's very close to the Canadian border. In fact, it's a six-hour drive from Mirror Falls, so pack your bags accordingly."

Lainey's jaw dropped open and she was glad he couldn't see the shock on her face.

"International Falls? She lives in International Falls?"

"You have a problem with that?"

"Oh, no," she muttered. "I was planning on a vacation trip to a lodge close to there. It took me by surprise, that's all."

"That's more convenient for you. You can keep your plans and enjoy a little down time…just not too much!" he chuckled. "We're still paying you to work, you know."

The two talked a few more minutes before ending their call. She hadn't been able to focus on the conversation after hearing where the case was located. Her mind filled with all kinds of thoughts.

In less than twenty-four hours, her plans to take the last week of December off to stay home and relax, not thinking about work at all, had been changed drastically by unexpected circumstances. Her rest and relaxation now meant becoming a housekeeping maid at Reindeer Lodge to help Shep's long-time friend, as well as investigating embezzlement and a possible murder case in International Falls. And she had only two days to prepare…and pack!

The call with Snoops had taken longer than expected. She checked her watch and hurried to shower and dress. Francy and Della would be at Babe's and she didn't want to be late. And boy - did she need a Mocha Frappe!

Lainey parked in the lot behind Babe's and met up with Della as she was walking inside. Francy was waiting at their favorite table.

"Hi, girls," Francy greeted, raising her hand to wave to them. "It's about time you got here. I had to run two people off who were trying to sit at our table!"

The friends laughed as Della and Lainey pulled out their chairs and sat down. The Whoopee group were regulars at Babe's and the running joke among the staff and fellow customers was that the last table on the right side by the restroom was considered reserved on the days the group usually came. Only unknown visitors would dare to consider sitting there on those days. The staff had referred to the table as the WGCT... Whoopee group coffee talk table. Vera had laughed when she first heard the name and said it should be called the gossip talk table instead.

"You three want the usual?" the server smiled as she walked toward the table. "Medium Mocha Frappe, medium iced Americano, and we have the Ho Ho Mocha Mint Christmas special, just for Della."

"Yum! I wait every year for the Ho Ho special to return! I'll take a large." Della licked her lips, rubbed her hands together, and grinned.

"Make my Mocha Frappe a large, too," Lainey chimed in. "I'm needing an extra boost this afternoon."

"Same here," Francy replied. "Large one, please."

"Coming right up!" The server smiled and walked away to place their order.

"I did some research last night and Reindeer Lodge was once a very popular destination," Francy commented as she dug into her purse that was hanging on the arm of her chair. "I printed off a couple of photos." She handed them to Della.

"It's a rustic log cabin style lodge and looks well kept," Della stated as she passed the photos to Lainey.

"The photos are ten years old," Francy answered. "The second photo shows the four individual cabins that are on the property."

"Wonder what happened that visitors stopped coming?" Della asked.

"I called Mom this morning to see if Shep had given her more details on why Mr. McAndrews is in financial trouble," Francy replied. "The only thing she mentioned was that he had lost everything because of investments he'd made after his wife passed away."

Lainey was quietly looking from one photo to another, not saying anything, her mind still preoccupied with the case she had been given that morning.

The server brought their drinks and said, "You gals are lucky today! Your coffee is free." She pointed to the front counter.

There stood Ben Sargent, the newly appointed captain of the Mirror Falls police department, smiling. He had worked with Francy for years before she retired and had been known as Sarge to his friends.

"Hey, Sarge! Come and sit with us," Francy called out.

He walked over, greeted the ladies, but didn't sit down.

"Good to see you are still occupying your table and supporting our local restaurants," he teased. "I wouldn't want to arrest you for loitering."

"Thank you for the coffees," Della said. "And congratulations on your promotion to Captain!"

"I guess we have to call you 'Cap' now!" Francy grinned. "Or would it be 'Sir Cap'?"

They laughed as his face turned red.

"No, Sarge is just fine," he chuckled. "I'm trying to get used to answering to 'Hey, Captain' around the office."

"Can you visit for a few minutes?" Lainey asked. "Tell us what's going on around town."

"Thanks, but I have to head back to the station. And as far as what's going on around town…you ladies probably know more than I do!" He winked. "Enjoy your coffee. Catch you later."

The three thanked him again and watched him walk out of the restaurant. They sipped their free coffees and turned their focus back to the lodge conversation.

"She's been unusually silent," Della said to Francy as she pointed to Lainey. "I think there's something going on that she hasn't shared with us."

"I was thinking the same thing," Francy nodded. "What's going on inside that head of yours?"

Lainey looked first at Francy, then Della, then

wiggled in her chair. They knew her too well. They would see through any excuse she came up with, so she let them in on her new case.

"Snoops from the home office assigned a case to me this morning," she began. "I'm…"

"Oh, no! You're not going with us! Darn those cases," Della interrupted. "So that means the Whoopee group of Merry Maids is down to two!"

Francy wasn't as quick to speak. She was watching Lainey's face and recognized her look of hesitation. She'd seen it many times before. Something odd was up with this recent case, so she phrased her question carefully.

"What's so special about this case?"

"It's not so much the case itself, it's where I have to go to investigate," Lainey replied. "International Falls." She watched as the concern on their faces turn into disbelief.

"No! You're kidding?" Francy questioned. "Minnesota's International Falls? The Icebox of the Nation?"

"That's right. And it's only a few miles from Reindeer Lodge."

Della sat back in her chair and gave a sigh of relief.

"Whew! I thought for a minute you weren't going with us."

Lainey nodded. She was still going but unsure of how much time she could spend cleaning cabins. Her smile had turned into a slight frown and Francy noticed.

"There's more to this case, isn't there?"

"Yes…well maybe," Lainey answered. She leaned forward and whispered. "It could be more than a fraud or embezzlement investigation. It could involve murder."

CHAPTER 4

Della and Francy stared at each other, then at Lainey. They had helped her with many cases and knew she was an intelligent, experienced investigator. But they also knew she was stubborn, adventurous, and often ran under the police radar…which put her in harm's way more times than she would admit.

"Since when do you get assigned to murder investigations? That's a far cry from embezzlement," Francy said with a matter-of-fact tone in her voice. She had witnessed many detectives investigate murders throughout her years in law enforcement. Some cases were cut and dried. Others took years to solve. Still others were never solved.

"Let me rephrase that," Lainey began, still whispering. "The case could *possibly* involve murder."

Della rolled her eyes. "Don't beat around the bush with us. Either it does or it doesn't."

"I won't have details until later this evening. For now, let's focus on getting ready to go to the Lodge day after tomorrow. I, for one, have a lot to do if I'm going to be gone for a month!"

"You're right," Francy replied as she reached into her purse again and took out her small iPad. "I'll take notes. Now, who is going to drive?"

The next hour went by quickly as the three discussed, laughed, and made plans for their trip. Della had a Cornhusker red Chevy Tahoe that had three rows and could hold up to nine people. They had teased her about the color many times. Friends said she was a magnet for speeding tickets or that Santa wanted his sleigh back or that astronauts could see her from the space station. She ignored their jokes. Nebraska was her favorite college football team and proudly displayed their college decals on the back window of the car.

They decided to meet early Friday morning at Della's, pack her Tahoe, and head up to Reindeer Lodge.

"Tomorrow's Thanksgiving and I've got to get home," Francy laughed. "Roger wants turkey and dressing with all the fixings…even giblet gravy!"

"Yuck." Della grimaced. "Paul calls that turkey innards juice. I think it's gross!"

The friends giggled, gathered their belongings, and headed out the door. As Lainey walked to her car, her mind was making a mental list of the chores to complete and items to pack.

I'm glad I don't have to cook a big turkey dinner. I'm happy heating Brussel sprouts with bacon bits and butter. Sometimes there are perks to being single!

She smiled as she got in her car and drove home.

The next day passed quickly and Lainey hardly had time to check her emails. She received the files from Snoops, as promised, but hadn't reviewed them. Instead, she printed only the two pages of details, intending to work on them on Friday's drive to the Lodge. Since she was taking her computer, she'd have access to them when she needed.

Her phone alarm sounded its loud rendition of "Under the Boardwalk" awakening her at 4 a.m. She yawned and sleepily walked into the kitchen to make a cup of coffee. Powie, her black cat, followed her and was stretching on the rug where she was standing.

"Powie, you're going to enjoy staying with Auntie Adriana for a few weeks. Her family spoils you rotten!" Lainey reached down to pick up the cat and give him a big hug. Adriana was her neighbor and had watched the cat when she was out of town for work. The teenager loved Powie and was coming later in the morning to gather up his food, bed, and favorite blanket.

"You be good for her," Lainey said, trying to sound like a parent. "Don't be bossy!"

Powie meowed as if he understood every word and then turned his head as if he was ignoring her.

She drank her coffee, showered, and was driving to Della's house before 6 a.m. Shep and Vera were already at the house, chomping at the bit to get on the road.

"Hey, Lainey," he greeted, giving her a hug. "Decided to sleep in, did you? We've been waiting for an hour."

"We have not," Vera scolded. "He's teasing you. I had to wake him up…" she stopped mid-sentence. "I mean, I had to call him to make sure he was up in time." She looked at Shep and he was grinning from ear to ear.

"I think she's old enough to know, Sweetie," he kidded. "Unless you want more details, Lainey?"

"No, no…" she replied, shaking her head and closing her eyes. "Some things are better left to the imagination!"

Francy arrived and the three were still laughing when she got out of her car.

"Are we having fun already?" she asked.

Shep looked at Vera and she gave him the evil eye, which meant to keep quiet. He didn't.

"I think you could say we had some fun, didn't we, you gorgeous woman, you!"

Vera winced, and even in the darkness of the morning, her cheeks were as red as Rudolph's nose.

Within thirty minutes, all suitcases, pillows, computers, snacks, and people were loaded into the two cars. Shep rolled down his window and called out to Della.

"Why don't you go first? I need a flashy red beacon to light my way in the dark." He chuckled.

She rolled down her window long enough to quip back. "Sure, you want me to get the speeding ticket, don't you?" She grinned, rolled up her window, and they were on their way.

Lainey sat in the front passenger seat with Francy sitting behind her. She plugged her computer into the 12V outlet on the Tahoe's dashboard and waited for it to connect.

"Did you get the case information last night?" Francy asked. "I'm ready to hear what's going on!"

"I haven't studied the all the files, but I do have the basic details."

She reached into the backpack that carried her laptop and pulled out the two pages she had printed.

"I am still shocked that the case is in International Falls," Della remarked.

"That makes two of us," Francy agreed. "You mentioned possibly a murder?"

Lainey nodded and snapped her fingers. "Oh shoot. I'd better set my phone alarm for 9:50 a.m. I'm supposed to call the client at 10."

She quickly set the alarm and began reading the

details out loud. Her company had received a call
from Mrs. Sadie Watson stating that Voyageurs
Financial Trust, LLC had employed her husband, Jake
Watson, for many years as an investment broker. A
few weeks ago, the owner of the company, Orson
Meade, discovered that hundreds of thousands of
dollars had been stolen from clients over two years.
Meade had accused Jake of stealing the money.
Apparently, Jake's explanation that he was being setup
by another employee fell on deaf ears. Meade fired
him and said he would prosecute him to the full
extent of the law.

Jake had gone home to their apartment feeling
crushed and depressed. Sadie had gone to work the
next day as usual and when she came home later that
evening, she found him lying dead on the kitchen floor.
The police report said it was a self-inflicted gunshot
wound, but Sadie refused to believe it. She says she has
proof he was being blackmailed, and that he was
innocent.

For a few moments, the only sound in the car was
the tires crunching the snow packed roads as they
pushed on toward Reindeer Lodge.

"My gosh," Della remarked. "This is much more
than embezzlement."

"I agree," Francy chimed in. "Are you to call this
Sadie Watson?"

"Yes. I'm to schedule a time to meet in person with

her. In fact, that's only a couple of minutes from now." She picked up her cell phone and turned off the alarm.

Francy thought for a moment and then spoke with her law enforcement tone of voice.

"Did Snoops tell you to contact the local authorities?"

Lainey shrugged her shoulders. "Not exactly...but if I thought it was murder, to let them have the information."

"Now, Miss Stubborn, you think I'm going to believe that?" Francy leaned forward to touch Lainey's shoulder.

"He said to contact them," she sighed heavily.

"And what else..."

"And that he was going to keep close tabs on me during this investigation." Lainey said hesitantly, then turned to look her friend squarely in the eyes. "Are you satisfied?"

"For now. I have a friend who works for the city of International Falls and I'm going to get the police chief's contact information just in case."

Lainey rolled her eyes and turned back to face the front of the car. She unlocked her cell phone and dialed the number she had for Sadie Watson. Once it began ringing, she hit the loud speaker button.

"Hello," a young woman's voice answered curtly.

"Hello. Is this Mrs. Watson?"

"Who are you?"

"I'm Lainey Maynard, the investigator Mr. Bedlow told you would call this morning."

There was a pause and what sounded like footsteps walking into a room and a door closing.

"At least you're prompt," the voice commented. "I'm Sadie. Can you meet with me this afternoon?"

Lainey blinked. "I'm on my way to International Falls and it would be early evening before I could meet."

"It's urgent that I see you…can you meet me at 6 p.m.?"

"I will do my best. Should I come to your home address?"

"No," the voice answered hurriedly. "I have your phone number. I'll text you the address. Have all the questions you need answered with you. I'm not sure how many more times I can see you."

"Yes, Ma'am. I will. Is there anything…"

"Look for a text and don't be late." The line went dead. Sadie had hung up.

For a moment, Lainey stared at her phone and no one in the car spoke.

Why would she hang up on me so abruptly? Who else was there?

"Wow. She's not the typical 'Minnesota Nice' personality, is she?" Francy frowned.

"It's obvious she's hiding something or someone," Della added.

Lainey's skin was tingling and thoughts were rapidly filling her mind with all kinds of scenarios… none of which were good. Her phone dinged, signaling a text message had arrived.

"She didn't sound like the grieving widow I expected to hear, either," she said as she unlocked her phone to read the message.

The text read: *3rd Street between 6th and 8th Avenues. Meet at Smokey Bear Park in front of the statue. I'll be wearing a deep purple coat and a stocking cap.*

"Smokey Bear Park?" Francy asked. "She wants to meet outside in a park?"

"I guess so. Good thing I brought my pocket recorder. I think I may need it sooner than I thought."

The conversation continued with many theories and comments. After only a couple of stops for gas and restroom breaks, the ladies found themselves outside the city limits of Ranier, Minnesota. It was close to 3 p.m.

"We made great time," Della announced. "And only two stops!"

"How much farther is the Lodge?" Francy asked. "I haven't seen a sign for it yet."

Lainey pulled up the GPS on her cell and searched for driving directions.

"According to my phone, we're only four miles away." She turned the volume up to the max so Della could hear the directions.

"At the fork, head south on County Road 20 onto County Road 113. At the four-way stop, cross MN 11 and continue straight until you arrive at your destination." The male voice directed.

"I think it's neat that your GPS voice is a male Brit!" Della giggled.

"I figured if someone was going to tell me where to go…I might as well enjoy it!"

"Hey," Francy questioned as she looked out the window. "Isn't that Big Vic, the Voyageur statue?"

"I think so," Lainey answered.

"In my humble opinion, Big Ole's statue in Alexandria is taller…and he has a spear and sword!"

They all laughed.

Della stopped at the intersection and looked across the road.

"Isn't that a sign for Reindeer Lodge? Do you see it? On the left."

She slowly drove across the intersection and headed for what looked like a sign shaped like a reindeer. The sign was worn, and the paint had faded, but the details of the reindeer were still visible. There were no words, but a large red plaid arrow pointing to the left.

"That's the same reindeer sign that is on the coffee cup Shep gave us," Francy said. "We must be headed to the right place."

Della turned the car onto the snow-covered road

where the arrow directed. The sides of the road were lined with tall trees whose leaves were scattered among the pine trees. A little further down the road, Christmas lights on either side stood like a fence, lighting the way. Just beyond was a large, curved sign that stretched from one side to the other. It twinkled with all colors of lights that outlined its border. On each end was a picture of the same coffee cup, only their lights were flashing off and on. The words in the middle read, 'Welcome Friends to Reindeer Lodge.' The letters of the word reindeer were shaped like antlers.

They drove under the sign and into a parking area in front of the two-story, rustic log cabin. The snow-covered roof had many unique shapes and angles that made the lodge resemble a regal wooden mansion. Christmas lights graced every pillar, roof line, window, and balcony. The entire building glowed in yellow, green, red, and blue.

Shep parked his car next to Della's, got out, and opened the door for Vera. Lainey, Francy, and Della were gathering their bags.

"What's your first impression of the lodge?" Shep said to the ladies.

"It's cozy and much larger than I thought," Francy answered. "I can't wait to see the inside."

"Remember why we are here. Jim has done his best to keep the place up, but it's going to need some work."

A narrow walkway to the front entrance had been

shoveled and salted. The porch wound its way around
the building and had wooden rocking chairs scattered
on it. As they got close to the tall front doors, a
handsome man opened one side and greeted them.

"Hello again, Shep! I'm so glad to see you."

"Hey, Kevin. Good to see you. Did you bring Jim
home?"

"I'm going to pick him up later this evening. Come
on in and let's get you settled."

He smiled and looked at Vera.

"Let me help you with your bags," he winked.
"Beautiful young ladies shouldn't be carrying their own
luggage!"

"You are just the sweetest thing," Vera laughed. "And
pretty darn cute, too, don't you think, Lainey?"

Startled, Lainey gave a nod and a half smile. She
wanted to crawl under one of the rocking chairs to
hide.

Here we go again...Vera the matchmaker.

Inside, Shep introduced everyone to Kevin
McAndrews, Jim's younger son. He was over six feet
tall, had broad shoulders, and was very muscular. His
reddish-brown beard and mustache complimented his
lumber jack plaid shirt. Lainey noticed his eyes were an
icy green and sparkled as brightly as the Christmas
lights outside. She had to admit he was every bit as cute
as Vera said.

The lodge was gorgeous. Large log beams held up

the ceiling of the lobby. Every wall had trophy mounts of deer, elk, and moose. A double fireplace made from multi-stone colored bricks extended from the floor to the ceiling in the center of the room. Around the fireplace were many little spots where visitors could sit. There were oversized puffy arm chairs covered in brown bear fabric, chairs that were made from antlers, and many end tables and coffee tables of various sizes and shapes.

On the floor were throw rugs with bears or moose on them. The focal point of the room was the front wall. Large windows filled the wall with a mantle dividing what would be the first and second floors. And in front of the grand windows was a waterfall fountain that flowed into a small pond. Inside the pond, standing on rocks that were built to look like a mountainside, was a large, dark brown stuffed moose. Its antlers were six feet across.

Christmas trees and decorations were everywhere, and the friends stood for a few moments, taking it all in.

"This is fantastic," Della said as she studied the pond display. "Did you build this?"

"Dad and I put this in just before my mom passed away. She loved nature, and this pond was something she had always wanted." Kevin answered rather sadly. "We do what we can to make Reindeer Lodge a place our guests want to call their home away from home."

"You've done an outstanding job," Francy acknowledged. "I can see where this would take more than two people to manage."

"We'd better get you to your rooms," Kevin said, motioning to the stairs. "We don't have an elevator, so follow me."

They each picked up their luggage and walked behind him. The stairway was wide, and the carpet had many worn spots. The log handrails were thick, round, and were also showing age from many years of dents and scratches from guests.

The main lodge had eight rooms on the second floor. Each room had an animal name and a wooden sconce with a little carved statue of that animal on it as a door light.

Francy took the Elvan Elk room, Della took the Monty Moose room, Lainey took the Andy Antelope room, and Vera and Shep took the Rudy Reindeer suite.

"I'll let you all get settled in. The cafe is on the first floor and tonight's dinner is deer stew. It will be ready around 6 p.m." Kevin said and turned to go back downstairs.

"Oh, I'm afraid I won't be able to come to dinner tonight," Lainey said. "I have an appointment in International Falls at that time."

Kevin paused. "I'm picking Dad up about that time. If Shep wouldn't mind dishing out the stew, you are welcome to ride to town with me."

The tingling Lainey usually felt when something was about to happen hit her like a ton of bricks.

Lainey...calm down. He's offering you a ride, that's all.

"I appreciate that, but I'm not sure how long I will be. I was going to ask to take Della or Shep's car."

"Nonsense, why waste gas. Why don't I meet you in the lobby at 5:30?"

Lainey hesitated. She was meeting a stranger in a city park in the winter at dark. Her instincts told her not to be without her own transportation.

"I appreciate the offer, but I will feel better having a car available when I need it."

"If that's what you want. Where is your meeting taking place?"

"In Smokey Bear Park."

Kevin's eyes opened wide, then narrowed quickly. "You're meeting at the statue...tonight?"

"Yes, why?"

"The Christmas Parade is tonight. There will be a lot of families and visitors lining the streets. Leave early to find a parking space."

Oh great. A parade with lots of people and no parking.

"Thank you for the warning. Do you know of a spot I could park?"

"The public library is across the street. It has a back parking lot for employees. You should be able to find a spot if you go early." He smiled, turned, and walked downstairs.

"Take my Tahoe," Della offered. "There is a flashlight in the glovebox, too."

Vera looked concerned. "I'd feel better if you were not alone. I'm coming with you."

"That's not necessary," Lainey smiled. "I appreciate the offer, but you need to stay here and help serve dinner."

"Okay, but I'm not a bit happy about it!"

They each went to their rooms to unpack and rest up. Lainey set up her computer to review the files on Sadie Watson. She noticed a new email from Snoops. The subject read 'Be careful of Christmas parade.' She shook her head and read the email. He knew she was meeting at the park and he was cautioning her about the annual parade occurring at the same time.

"How does he get this information so quickly?" she said aloud.

Her stomach was still queasy, and she wondered if the woman was setting her up. Meeting in a park during an annual parade with tons of visitors was out of the ordinary, to say the least.

She plugged in her cell phone to charge. The last thing she needed was to be without a way to call for help.

CHAPTER 5

L ainey focused on the case files Snoops had sent. A brief bio of Sadie Springer Watson and Jake Watson gave her insight to their backgrounds and upbringings. While both grew up in the area, their family environment was as different as night and day.

Ian and Elvina Springer adopted five children, of which Sadie was the youngest, through a Christian home for unwed mothers. Ian worked for the local paper mill and moonlighted as a janitor at the school. Elvina ran a small alterations business from her home, making all of her family's clothes to save money. She took jobs sewing for wedding attendants or brides in order to help make ends meet. Raising five children was expensive, and the couple struggled. Ian retired and passed away from lung cancer shortly after. Elvina was devastated and never fully recovered. She passed away one year after her husband. The siblings had extremely limited contact with each other from that time on.

Sadie struggled to graduate from high school as learning did not come easy for her. Instead of joining the school choir, band, or other clubs, she went home after class for additional study time. Her mom taught her to sew as a safety net if she couldn't get a better job. She briefly attended an area community college and worked at several convenience stores before landing a job as a front desk clerk for one of the hotels in town.

Louis and Tammy Watson had one child, Jake. Louis received a Mechanical Engineering degree from the University of Minnesota and worked his way up inside Cargill. He retired as Vice President of their Agricultural Products Division. Tammy's degree was in elementary education and she had been a fourth-grade teacher her entire career. She retired and the couple moved to Florida to enjoy the warmer climate.

Jake was intelligent, outgoing, and a natural athlete. He excelled in mathematics, science, and every sport he played. He'd earned the honor of salutatorian in his high school graduating class and received a degree in business and finance from his father's alma mater. Orson Meade, owner of Voyageurs Financial Trust, had hired Jake, who quickly became Orson's most valued employee.

Lainey stopped reading to check the time. It was close to 4 p.m. and she wanted to leave for Smokey Bear Park before 5. She quickly scanned down the pages, looking for the explanation of how the two met or fell in love.

Jake had met Sadie while he was visiting a friend who was staying at the hotel where she worked. They dated for a few months before getting married.

Lainey took a deep breath, closed her computer, stood up, and stretched. As she touched up her makeup to get ready for her meeting, she spoke out loud, going over what she had read.

"I'm surprised the files had little to say about how these two met. I know opposites attract more often than not, but the sound of Sadie's cold, callous voice this morning and her abruptness makes me suspicious."

Lainey put on her coat, placing her recorder in her pocket, and grabbed the keys Della had given her earlier that afternoon. It was already dark and she wasn't familiar with the roads or the town of International Falls. Kevin had warned her to leave early and she had to trust what he said. She locked the room door before heading downstairs.

"Did you change your mind about going with me?" Kevin smiled at her from behind the registration desk.

"No, but I am taking your advice to leave early. I hope there will be a parking space at the library."

"One of my buddies works close to the library. He

always parks there for the parade. I asked him to watch for your red car. He'll find you a space."

Lainey grinned. "Why thank you! You've got more connections than you let on."

"Nah…the guy owes me a favor, that's all."

His green eyes felt like lasers drilling deep into her soul. She shivered slightly and hoped he hadn't seen it.

"Well," she stammered. "I better be going."

Trying to walk out the door felt awkward, as if her legs didn't want to work. Once she was safely in the car, she rolled her eyes and took a couple of deep breaths.

What in the world is wrong with me? I'm probably too old for him anyway!

She started the car, rolled her shoulders and neck, programed the GPS, and adjusted the rearview mirror before heading to the park. The British male voice gave directions and within ten minutes, she drove past the city limits sign of International Falls. Immediately, a line of traffic made her slow down to a crawl. Cars crept along the road, all trying to find a parking place to view the parade.

Lainey tapped her thumbs on the steering wheel, watching the clock on the dashboard tick away the minutes. The last thing she needed was to be late for her meeting with Sadie.

Finally, the GPS showed the library building was a

few blocks away on her left. She turned in slowly, looking for any open parking space.

"I wish Kevin had told me what this guy looked like," Lainey mumbled out loud.

She drove through the front lot and followed the paved road to the back of the building. Sitting on the tailgate of a Dodge Ram pickup truck was a man wearing a heavy brown Carhartt coat, an orange vest, and an orange stocking cap. He motioned for her to pull into the space on his left. She parked carefully and got out to thank him.

He had jumped off the tailgate and walked around the Tahoe to meet her.

"Thank you, sir," she said, extending her hand to shake his. "I appreciate your help so much."

"No problem, Ma'am," he said, shaking her hand. "Around here we help people out when we can."

"My name's Lainey Maynard and I'm thankful Kevin got in touch with you. I wasn't expecting a Christmas parade this evening!"

The man had a look of confusion on his face. He paused briefly, then recovered his friendly expression.

"I'm Sven Jorgensen. I think Kevin said you were meeting someone at the statue this evening? If you're going to watch the parade, that's not the best spot to see it."

"That's good to know," she blurted, not wanting to

share any information about who or why she was
meeting.

"You want to make sure you see Santa and his
sleigh. It's the Lodge's rig and the highlight of the
parade."

"Reindeer Lodge has a sleigh?"

"Yes, and four not so tiny reindeer. You're staying at
the lodge, right? Be sure Kevin takes you on a sleigh
ride. It comes with blankets and hot cocoa!"

The two laughed. She thanked him again and
walked over to the park across the street. The Smokey
Bear statue was hard to miss. It was in the center of the
little park and was in the middle of a circular brick
sidewalk. Standing on a pedestal painted to resemble a
tree trunk, Smokey's right hand was raised as if to say
'stop'. He held a large shovel in his left hand. Two small
bears, one hugging each of his huge legs, served as his
helpers. His famous saying was carved into the
pedestal; Smokey says, "Prevent Forest Fires."

The sound of car horns, people cheering, and
holiday music floated through the air as the parade
drew closer. Lainey looked at her watch. It was 5:55.
She saw no one wearing a purple coat or standing
anywhere near the statue.

She stood in front of the big bear, switching her
weight from one foot to the other to keep them warm.
Five minutes passed, then ten. Still no sign of Sadie.
She took her cell phone from her pocket and played the

solitaire game she had downloaded to kill time. She would wait till 6:30 before leaving.

The snow was crunching behind her when she heard the voice. She turned to see a woman dressed in a shiny purple winter coat and matching stocking cap. She fought the urge to greet the woman with the words 'You're late'.

"You must be Mrs. Watson," she said, holding out her hand. "I'm Lainey Maynard."

"I know who you are," the woman answered. It was obvious she was nervous. She turned her head from side to side to see if anyone else was watching or listening. "I told your boss my thoughts. What are you going to do about this?"

"I need more information in order to start this investigation." She had lowered her hand into her pocket and gently turned on the recorder she had hidden there.

The woman looked around again and unzipped her coat. When she put her hand in to pull something out, Lainey's guard went up.

"Hold on, what are you reaching for?" she questioned, and backed up a few steps.

"Relax. It's the proof I told you I had." She took out a large manilla envelope. "Take this. It will tell you all you need to know." She looked around for the third time. "I have little time. If you need to contact me, use the number I texted to you."

Lainey stepped forward, taking the envelope from her.

"Sadie, is someone watching you? Are you afraid for your safety? The police can…"

"I'm fine. My husband was innocent. Do your job. I've given you enough information. Find the person who embezzled the money. He's Jake's killer."

"Wait! I can help you!" But the woman turned and started running into the darkness behind the statue.

Not familiar with the area, Lainey knew she couldn't follow her at night. She looked at the envelope and back where the woman had just been standing. The footprints she left in the snow disappeared into the darkness.

The crowd noise was growing louder and louder as she walked back across the street to the library. The song 'Here Comes Santa Claus' was blasting through loud speakers, signaling the arrival of Santa and his sleigh…and the end of the parade. She grinned, remembering the excitement she felt as a little girl, watching her town's parade and hoping the man in the red suit would wave to her.

She walked around the back of the building toward her car and noticed a familiar figure standing close to the Tahoe.

"Sven?" she called out. "Are you still here? I thought you were watching the parade?"

"I saw the parade. I must have reached my truck just

before you rounded the corner of the building. Were you able to catch any of the floats?"

"My friend was late and I'm afraid we missed the parade. But I can hear that Santa was a big hit once again this year."

The man nodded. "The traffic will be lighter if you leave town the back way. Why don't you follow me? I'll get you to the main road back to the Lodge. It will save you an hour's time and you won't be sitting in traffic."

"That's very kind of you. Thanks so much. I'll try to stay close to your truck so I don't lose you."

"Few people drive a Tahoe that's a louder color than the sun at high noon. I will not lose you." He chuckled.

She smiled. He was right! She got in her car and followed the Dodge Ram out of the parking lot. The GPS, programmed to return the same way as she came, was trying to recalculate with every turn the Tahoe made. Sure enough, within a few minutes, Sven had taken her to the main highway, avoiding all the tired parade goers and their cars. She waved goodbye and headed to the Lodge.

Lainey walked into the lobby as the grandfather clock standing behind the registration desk struck 8. She could hear voices coming from the hallway that led to the cafe.

"I am hungry," she said aloud as she started walking down the narrow corridor. She marveled at the paintings that hung on the walls. They were in a sequence, the first one making you think you were walking into a snowy forest. As you walked past the next paintings, it was as if you were walking deeper and deeper into the woods. Several had reindeer and elk scattered among the trees. The hallway ended at the cafe entrance and the last painting showed the forest running in to a log cabin looking very similar to the Lodge itself. A carved wooden sign above the door read 'Bella's Cafe.'

She walked inside to see Shep bartending and washing glasses behind the small bar. Della, Francy, and Vera were sitting at the bar eating and talking.

"Glad to see you made it back from the parade route," he mused. "I was beginning to think elves who thought the Tahoe was Santa's red sleigh had kidnapped you."

"Santa would love to ride in a sleigh like my Tahoe!" Della fired back quickly. "And his bag of toys would fit nicely in the back."

"Smells good in here. Do you have any of the stew left, Shep?" Lainey asked as she sat down on the stool next to Vera.

"You bet. I'll bring you a bowl. There's homemade cornbread, too. Want some honey to go with it?"

"You know me too well. Thank you!"

Vera leaned close to her, giving her a one-handed hug. "We're glad you're back safely, but what happened with the grumpy widow lady?"

Shep appeared from the kitchen carrying a steaming bowl of stew, two pieces of cornbread, and a bottle of fresh honey on a tray. He sat it down in front of Lainey, then looked at Vera.

"Give her a second to eat and warm up before you grill her with questions," he commented. "She's too thin to be skipping supper."

"Oh, Piddle," Vera grunted, waving her hand toward him as if to swat his remark away like a nuisance fly.

"He's right, Mom," Francy grinned and looked over at Lainey. "But couldn't you eat a little bit faster?"

They were laughing when Kevin came through the entrance, pushing a man in a wheelchair. Shep hurried from behind the bar to greet them.

"Jim! Boy, it's good to see you!" he stretched out his hand to shake the man's uninjured left hand.

"I'm glad to be here at all." His smile turned into a wide grin, and his top lip began to quiver. "I can't thank you enough for…"

"Now we talked about this. No thanks needed. We've been buddies for a long time. You'd do the same for me."

Tears formed in Jim's eyes and he blinked several times to keep them from escaping and streaming down his cheeks. Kevin nodded to Shep showing his appreciation and patted his dad on the shoulder.

"Dad, you know Vera. She's been a big help already today."

"Hello, Vera. Good to see you again. Are you still keeping that old man under control?"

"You look terrific, Jim," Vera said, standing up from the bar stool. She walked over and bent to give him a hug. Then she stood up and put both her hands on her hips and sighed.

"How you ever kept that old Swede in line during the service is nothing short of an act of courage…or a way to keep your sanity!"

"He can be a bit stubborn, but he's the best darn cook on the planet!"

Shep shrugged his shoulders, lifted his hands and stated proudly, "Was there ever any doubt about that?"

Once the laughter died down, Kevin pushed Jim closer to the bar where the ladies were sitting.

"And you must be the Whoopee group I've been told so much about," Jim said. "Now, who is who?"

The three ladies each stood up, taking turns walking over to greet him.

"I'm Della Kristiansen. It's so nice to meet you."

"Hello Mrs. Kristiansen."

"Please, all my friends call me Della."

"Thank you," Jim nodded. "Let me see if I can guess which one of you two ladies is Vera's daughter." He put his hand up to his chin as if in deep thought.

Francy raised her hand. "Guilty as charged!" she confessed.

"I can see the family resemblance," he answered. "I know she's very proud of you."

"Let's just say she puts up with me…" she laughed. "Nice to meet you, Jim. Please, call me Francy."

Lainey had been smiling and listening, grabbing small bites of cornbread while she waited her turn to be introduced.

"And Dad, this is Lainey Maynard," Kevin began. "She's the investigator you were told about."

"It's nice to meet you, sir." She greeted Jim with a hug, like the others. "But who told you I was an investigator?" She raised her eyebrows and narrowed her eyes at Vera and Shep.

Vera rolled her eyes and pointed to Shep, who was trying to sneak back behind the bar.

"Don't think you can hide!" Vera called out to him.

"It's okay," Lainey winked. "I'll forgive you this time."

The group talked for several more minutes about their trip to the Lodge, how beautifully decorated it was, and the great stew for their supper.

"Believe it or not," Jim said, yawning. "Kevin made the dinner tonight. He can cook when he wants to."

Kevin frowned slightly. "It's been a busy day, Dad. I think it's time to take you up to the room and get you settled in for the night."

"I am tired. I hope you all will excuse me as my son

tucks me into bed!" He grinned. His tiredness shown in his eyes.

Kevin turned the wheelchair around and was heading toward the door when his dad stopped him to whisper something in his ear. The son nodded and obediently turned the wheelchair around once more to face their new friends.

"I know you are here to help clean up this place," he started speaking when his voice broke. It took a few seconds for him to regain his composure. "I will never be able to thank you. This lodge, it was our dream, Peg and me. She was my rock, my direction, my entire world. When she died…" he lowered his head. This time, he couldn't stop the tears from flowing.

Shep once again walked over to his friend and laid his hand on his shoulder. Each person's heart was breaking and the silence in the air said everything.

"Jim, things are going to be fine. The best thing you can do is rest."

Tears slipped out of Kevin's eyes as he turned his dad's chair around to leave the room.

"Thank you," the son said gratefully. "I'll see you all in the morning."

CHAPTER 6

Everyone had tears in their eyes as they watched Jim leave the cafe. They were quiet for a few minutes, trying to regroup their thoughts for the next day. Shep was behind the bar getting ready to close for the evening and the ladies were setting on the bar stools. As he closed the cash register, he picked up a clipboard and walked toward the ladies at the counter.

"Kevin was kind enough to make a list of the daily duties that need to be taken care of. We need to decide who is going to do what."

He passed the clipboard around so that each one could choose their chores. Vera spoke up first.

"Do we know how many guests are arriving and when to expect them? Kevin mentioned he would handle the check in/check out each day."

"I believe he mentioned they had four couples arriving at the end of next week. That means we have about five days to get things cleaned, polished, and spit-shined for them!"

Vera handed Francy the clipboard. "This list says there are four cabins, all which need cleaning. That is, besides the rooms inside the lodge," she stated. "You girls need to choose which ones you want to tackle. Shep and I will help, but the kitchen and food service are our major focus."

"In my younger days," Della began, "I worked my way through college as a hotel maid. I'm fine with taking the rooms inside the lodge. Besides, I'm not fond of tramping around in four-foot snowdrifts taking cleaning supplies to a cabin."

"How far do you think these cabins are from the main lodge?" Lainey asked, motioning for Francy to pass the clipboard. "I didn't see any cabins when we first arrived."

"I'm not sure," Shep answered. "Kevin will have to show you tomorrow. They can't be that far away. People do have to come to the main lodge to eat, right?"

"Maybe these cabins have small kitchenettes in them. That would make sense." Della added.

Lainey nodded. "Wonder if Jim or Peg named these cabins? I think they were very creative!"

"How about I take two of the cabins, and Lainey, you take the other two. I know you're working on the case…hey, that reminds me! What did you find out with Sadie?" Francy questioned.

"She was late and still very brash." She didn't want to go into details until she had looked at the envelope. "I can tell you all about it in the morning. Which cabins do you want?"

Francy wiggled her mouth from side to side, trying to decide. She tapped her chin with her fingers and then giggled. "I'll take the Voyageurs Cabin and the Northwoods Cabin. Since they are cabins 1 and 2, I won't have to walk as far!"

"Guess that leaves me with Snowy Woods Cabin and Caribou Cabin," she grinned. "I might have farther to walk, but I know something you don't…and I'm not telling!"

Della leaned forward. "Something exciting? You know I love surprises!"

"No…well, maybe exciting," Lainey laughed. "Reindeer Lodge has a sleigh and four not so tiny reindeer."

"How do you know that?" Francy asked.

"One of Santa's elves told me that the sleigh and reindeer carrying old Saint Nick in the parade tonight were owned by the lodge."

"You can bet I'm not cleaning out those stalls!" Vera spouted, shaking her head. "No shoveling old reindeer poop for me!"

"You'd probably scare the antlers off of them

anyway," Shep teased. "I'm the only old poop you better have contact with!"

Vera's face flushed. "Oh…you're…you're…"

"Adorable? Handsome? A real sweetie?" he grinned.

"You're impossible!"

The ladies chuckled. It was nice to see Vera and Shep happy. Both had lost their spouses years ago and even though they sometimes fought like cats and dogs, it was clear how much they cared for each other.

"What time can we meet for breakfast?" Della asked. "I think we should hit the sack tonight and regroup in the morning."

"It's a continental breakfast and I plan to have it ready at 6 a.m.," Shep answered.

"Sounds good. I'm heading up to my room. Sleep tight all." Francy stood up, stretched, and yawned.

"Night everyone," Lainey replied. She was eager to get to her room and see what the envelope contained.

The ladies left the cafe and walked upstairs. After saying goodnight one more time, Lainey unlocked her room and stepped inside. To her surprise, and delight, there was a small vase of pink carnations sitting on the desk. The card read 'To the Whoopee Merry Maids Service, From your favorite chef.'

Shep had somehow managed to get flowers for each of them without their knowledge.

He is a good man. I'm glad Vera met him!

Lainey sat at the desk, turned on her computer, and

carefully opened the envelope from Sadie. Inside were several papers stapled together and a photograph. She studied the papers and immediately the familiar tingling sensation kicked in. Her intuition told her to be cautious with the information in her hand.

The pages of the stapled stack appeared to be printed copies of invoices, a receipt, and pages from Excel spreadsheets. This wasn't the first time she had investigated an embezzlement case, and she noticed the letterhead on each invoice was slightly different. They were indeed from Voyageurs Financial Trust, but the spacing on the font of the address was not uniform. That was the first red flag.

One tool that Lainey always carried in her backpack was a magnifying glass. It had come in handy many times over the years. She used it to examine the receipt. It was for a $15,000 payment into a retirement fund. A white out strip had been placed over the original name of the client and clear tape had been used to cover it up with a new name inserted. Red flag number two.

There was nothing extraordinary about the photograph. A man dressed in what appeared to be a blue business suit was walking away from an auto dealership. The photo was taken from a distance away and the details of the man's face were not clear. She'd have to dig into this further before it could reveal anything.

Last, the spreadsheet was interesting. It contained client account numbers, but no names. The Voyageurs agent number was highlighted in yellow. Each column was labeled as a certain investment type with a total at the bottom. Lainey took a deep breath when she saw the accumulated total of all the columns…well over $50,000,000 dollars.

She put the papers down and leaned back in the chair. Questions raced through her mind.

"Did Sadie alter these pages? How did she get this information? From Jake's office files? Who's the guy in the photo?" she said aloud. But why Sadie had been nervous when they met earlier in the evening puzzled her the most. "Wonder if someone had been following her?"

She sat forward in the chair, put her hands on the keyboard and searched for Voyageurs Financial Trust. Instantly, pages of results appeared. The first few were ads for other financial resources. Lainey scrolled down to find the actual website for the company and clicked on it.

The home page looked very impressive and professional. The header was a photograph of Voyageurs National Park with the company logo proudly displayed on the left. She noticed the logo was different from the one on the invoices, proving to her that someone had tampered with them.

She clicked on the tab that said <u>Meet our Staff</u>. The

photo of Founder and CEO Orson Meade portrayed him as a handsome and sophisticated gentleman… Someone who future clients could trust. Lainey typed his email and direct phone number into her phone. She would call him first thing in the morning to make an appointment. She scrolled down to see a photo of a mid-30's good-looking guy named Jake Watson. The picture was the usual professional head shot, and he had that all-American-generally-nice-guy smile and appearance.

Lainey frowned and leaned closer to the computer screen as the next agent's photo appeared. The man was about the same age as Jake. He was sitting behind an expensive-looking desk with his hands clasped together in front of him. What appeared to be awards or plaques were placed close by him. On the wall behind him was a photo of two men standing on a golf course.

Using the magnifying glass, she saw that the golf course was the TPC Twin Cities in Blaine, MN. One man in the golf photo was the agent, and the other was Tony Finau, the 3M Open golf champion of 2022.

Lainey blinked a few times and stared at the photo. The name of the agent was Andy McAndrews. No one had mentioned the name of Jim's older son, but could it be a coincidence that this guy had the same last name? She put his name, email, and direct number into her phone as well.

She turned her gaze once more to the screen. Andy was wearing a blue business suit…similar to the man's suit in the photograph Sadie had given her.

It was close to 10 p.m. Lainey closed the computer and turned on the television to watch the news and weather before heading to bed. She hadn't realized how tired she was, and fell asleep during the newscast.

She awoke early the next morning to the sound of the local news station giving the morning's drive and weather forecast. Her phone alarm sounded, letting her know it was 4:30 a.m. She rubbed her eyes, sat on the edge of the bed, then rubbed her neck. Her thoughts turned to the day ahead and the information she had learned last evening.

It didn't take her long to shower and dress. Sadie's information and the photo of Andy McAndrews kept running through her mind. As she walked down the stairs to meet the others in Bella's Cafe for breakfast, she had planned out her next steps, totally forgetting about cleaning any cabins.

"Morning, Shep!" Lainey called out as she walked into the cafe and sat down at a table. "Thank you for the carnations."

"Good morning to you, too." He walked over and gave her a big hug. "I'm glad you liked the flowers."

He wore was his favorite old white apron that had a faded logo of the Backwater Restaurant on the upper right pocket. The saying 'Never Trust a Skinny Chef' covered the middle section in red and black script that looked hand written.

"How about I bring you a coffee while we wait for the others?"

"That sounds wonderful. The lodge wouldn't happen to offer specialty coffee, say a Mocha Frappe , would they?"

"I've got you covered. No machine, but there are many ways to skinny a Frappe!"

Lainey was laughing when her friends walked in.

"You are perky this morning, Ms. Maynard," Francy grinned. "Would that be because you received flowers from a certain chef like we did?"

"That was so sweet of Shep," Della smiled. "He's a good catch for sure!"

"Agreed!" Lainey nodded, pointing to the chairs around the table. "Have a seat. Have you seen your Mom this morning?"

"Isn't she here cooking with Shep?" Francy asked. "I didn't stop by her room. I figured she would be here bossing the cook!"

"I gave her the breakfast shift off," Shep said, putting a Mocha Frappe in front of Lainey. "It's not Starbuck's, but I think you'll like it."

Picking up the mug of blended chocolate coffee, Lainey smiled. "It smells heavenly!"

"And what would you two ladies like? Coffee? Orange juice? I'm here to serve."

"Coffee with cream and sugar for me," Francy said. "Della, do you want OJ?"

"Only if it is in a mimosa! I didn't sleep a wink last night." She sighed heavily.

"I might concoct something akin to a mimosa." He bowed slightly and walked back to kitchen.

"Was something wrong with your room?" Lainey asked. "Normally, you're the first one to sleep and the last one to get up."

"It's strange, but I swear I heard voices underneath my window several times. Then I'd hear a thud or knock or something. And I had the distinct feeling that someone was watching me."

"We're on the second floor," Francy questioned. "How could you hear voices under the window?"

Della shook her. "I've got no clue. I think I'm going crazy. But I heard bumps and noise all night."

"What makes you think you were being watched?"

"Just a feeling, that's all. Do you have pictures in your bathroom?"

Lainey and Francy looked at each other and both shrugged.

"To be honest, I didn't look that closely. I know there is a big mirror over the sink." Francy said.

"I don't remember a picture *in* the bathroom, but there is one across from the bathroom door." Lainey replied. "Why? What picture do you have?"

"It's a black-and-white photo of someone holding a

big camera in front of their face, pointing it at me like they are going to take a picture." She grimaced. "It sounds silly, I know. But I felt like someone really was looking through that lens watching me."

Shep had returned with a steaming cup of coffee and a glass of orange juice.

"Try this. It's not champagne, but I found a skinny beer in the refrigerator."

Della took a sip, then a big gulp, and grinned. "Ah... a beer-mosa! That'll perk me up!"

"Or put you to sleep, silly," Francy laughed. "You're such a big drinker!"

"I can't put my finger on what is bothering me about the room. I'm going to go through it with a fine-toothed comb right after breakfast."

"Crime-a-nellie!" Lainey blurted out. "I completely forgot about cleaning those cabins! I have to call Orson Meade and get him to see me sometime today."

"Will you tell us now what information you received from Sadie...what was her last name again?" Francy asked.

"Watson. Sadie Watson. She gave me some papers and a photo, but I'm certain those papers have been altered. That's why it is imperative I see Orson Meade today, if at all possible."

"Orson Meade? Who is that?" Vera walked into the cafe and caught the tail end of the conversation as she walked over to their table.

"He's the owner of Voyageurs Financial Trust in International Falls. That's where Jake Watson was employed and the man who accused him of embezzlement." Lainey finished her frappe, setting the cup on the table and saw Kevin coming in the door.

"Morning all," he greeted. "Hope you slept well. Smells good in here, Shep. I'm hungry!"

"I made scrambled eggs, bacon, and biscuits with sausage gravy. There's also those packaged muffins and bagels you had in the refrigerator. Help yourselves!"

The group devoured the home cooked food and left the prepackaged items alone. As they sat around the table eating, the conversation focused on the tasks Kevin needed completed.

"The two families we have in the lodge will check out this morning. If those rooms could be cleaned, that would be a huge help." He said. "Have you divided up the chores?"

"Yes, they did," Vera chimed in. "Della's our head lodge housekeeping guru. Francy will be in charge of the cabins 1 and 2, and Lainey will work on cabins 3 and 4."

"And Vera is here to make sure I do my job her way," Shep smiled. "Isn't she just a cutie this morning?" He gave her a kiss on the cheek and a hug.

"You old goat," Vera grinned, obviously enjoying the hug and the attention.

"Well, I think the old goat is the best cook and

bottle-washer around," Kevin laughed, rubbing his stomach. "That's the best breakfast I've had in a long time. Thank you, Shep."

"It's my pleasure," the chef replied. "Your dad left a chart for me, showing the days of the week and about how many lunches, dinners, and other meals he would plan for. We know guests are arriving at the end of the week. How many walk-ins do you plan on? Do locals come for dinner?"

"During the week, we might have one or perhaps two people check-in for a night's stay. We might have three or four couples come by for Friday or Saturday night to eat…" he paused. A sadness came over his face. "Since Mom passed away, Covid hit, and food has become so expensive, we've lost most of our regulars."

Shep nodded. "I understand. I noticed there was not a lot of food in the freezer. How about I put together a new menu with some standard dishes. Vera and I will take care of purchasing the food. Think Jim will approve?"

The smile on Kevin's face was one of gratitude. "He trusts you. Why don't you talk to him about how much to buy? The lodge is to be listed for sale on January first."

"I'll do that after I clean up from breakfast."

"Thanks. My work isn't getting done while I'm sitting here!" He stood up, pushed his chair under the table, and turned to leave.

"Say Lainey," he said as an afterthought. "Did my friend help you last evening?"

"He did. And he helped me avoid the traffic after the parade concluded."

"Sven knows all the back roads around these parts."

"He also mentioned your reindeer. I saw from the Lodge's website that you provided sleigh rides, but I assumed you had horses."

A big grin spread across Kevin's face. "We've had reindeer since Mom and Dad bought the lodge. You want to walk with me to meet them? I feed them about this time each morning."

"Yes, she would," Francy answered for her. "She needs to find out how far the two cabins she needs to clean are from the lodge."

"Why, yes, that would be great," Lainey muttered. She squinted her eyes at her friend as if to say *thanks a bunch*. "Let me grab a few things and I'll meet you in the lobby, okay?"

"See you shortly," he replied, walking out of the cafe.

"And you, my busy-body friend," she glared at Francy. "You need to find your cabins, too. Get your coat, I'm not letting you out of this one!"

"Hold on," Della interrupted. "She promised to help me investigate the noises I heard from my room last night."

"That's right," Francy nodded. She winked at Della. "Those noises are my priority!"

"Sure it is. This looks like a setup to me," Lainey smiled as she stood up to leave. "Fair warning. I expect to hear what you found when I get back this afternoon!"

The two nodded, and as she turned to leave, she heard them giggling.

Good friends, huh? They're as bad as Vera at matching making!

CHAPTER 7

The morning was cloudy and gray, and a foggy mist hung in the air, making the Christmas lights on the lodge appear mystical. Kevin and Lainey walked outside into the cold. The wind was picking up and both were dressed to stay warm.

"Brr," Lainey said, making sure her stocking cap was snuggly covering her ears. "That wind is going to be brutal today."

"The trees surrounding the lodge give us some protection, but it's not unusual for December windchills to be well below zero."

The only sound as the two walked toward a snow-packed path that led into a group of pine trees was their boots crunching on the frozen ground. Lainey looked around trying to create a mental picture of the lodge's property.

The road curved and on the right-hand side was a large barn. Christmas lights similar to those at the lodge outlined the wooden walls. The barn's faded red paint showed years of wear from the harsh winter weather. The same reindeer shaped sign that had been on the main road to the lodge hung above the sliding door. It read 'Welcome Friends to Bella's Stable.'

"Do you have a relative named Bella? Or is there some family connection to the name?" Lainey asked when they stopped in front of the barn.

"Bella was the first reindeer my folks owned," he chuckled. "Actually, they didn't own her. They found her on the property when they purchased it. She had been abandoned without food or water, and my folks nursed her back to health. I guess you can say Bella adopted them."

He tugged at the wooden door to slide it open. "Sometimes, my brother and I thought she was treated better than we were!" He walked inside and motioned for Lainey to follow.

"Bella and my dad walked the property every day. She followed him as he did his chores, and he would talk to her as if she was his best friend. When she died many years later, it was as if we'd lost a family member. That's when Mom named the cafe after her."

This was the first time Lainey had seen a happiness

in Kevin. He walked through the stalls, patting, talking, and introducing each reindeer to her.

"These are Bella's grandchildren," he began. "Ivan is the oldest...and the leader of our sleigh team."

"Hello, Ivan," she said, putting her hand out to stroke his forehead. The reindeer grunted and startled her. She pulled her hand back quickly.

"Don't mind him. He's a push-over once he gets to know you."

He introduced her to Thor and Elof, the other two males, and stopped in front of the last stall.

"And this princess is Zella. She's the last of Bella's bloodline." If reindeer smiled, Zella's was huge as he stroked her forehead.

"She certainly loves you," Lainey remarked.

"Well, I'm a bit partial to her," he said as Ivan raised his head, grunting loudly in disapproval.

"You're special, too, old boy." Kevin shouted. "Don't be so jealous!"

The reindeer snorted and turned his back to the front of the stall.

"Let me feed them and then we can walk to the cabins."

Lainey watched as he filled the trough in each of the stalls, talking to each reindeer. She noticed how relaxed he was. His eyes sparkled...and that made her smile.

"All fed for today," he said as he put the feed bucket back on its shelf.

A question had been filling her thoughts since Kevin had mentioned his brother. She waited till they were outside the barn and heading down the snowy path to the cabin area before she spoke.

"Shep told us that Jim had two sons. Does your brother live close by?"

The happiness she had seen on his face faded instantly and a sense of disgusted anger took its place.

"I'm not close to my older brother," he said coldly. "My Mom was the glue that kept things civil between us."

"Oh, I didn't mean to bring up bad feelings," she apologized. Shutting off communication with him was the last thing she wanted to do.

He shrugged and they walked quietly for a few minutes.

"Andy and I have always been direct opposites of each other. He wanted a fancy corporate lifestyle while I enjoy living a simple life."

Lainey forced herself to keep walking and not grill him with questions.

"Your brother's name is Andy?"

He nodded.

"Does he live close to here?" she hesitated, not wanting to dig too deep.

He nodded again, walking a few more steps before answering.

"Andy lives in International Falls…when he isn't traveling the globe trying to impress people."

He stopped and turned to face her.

"I'm the one that needs to apologize," he began. "He wasn't around when Mom died and he rarely comes by the lodge to see Dad. I tend to get angry and defensive when I think about it."

"I'm sorry, Kevin. That must be tough."

"It's not your fault."

They started walking toward a fork in the path. His mood shifted and when he looked at Lainey, the angry expression was gone.

"Guests know when they come to the fork in the path, two cabins lie on either side." He walked over and wiped snow off the home-made sign shaped like a big wooden fork. On the handle of the fork were two arrows, similar to the arrow on the highway sign.

Lainey walked closer to read the thin signs. Voyageurs and Northwoods were on the right. Snowy Woods and Caribou were on the left.

"Great! I'll tell Francy what to look for when she comes to clean her cabins."

"They are pretty easy to find. The cabins are painted green and stand within fifty yards of each other, depending on which side of the fork you take. Ready to see your two cabins?"

The time had gone by quickly and she still had to call Orson Meade. She looked at her watch before answering.

"Can we do a raincheck? I have to make a few phone calls and I need to get back to the lodge."

"Of course," the right side of his mouth raised up slightly. "I took more of your time than I had intended."

They started walking back toward the lodge. Kevin stopped in front of the barn.

"Do you mind going on ahead? I've chores to do, one of which is cleaning out the stalls."

"Thank you for taking your time to introduce me to your reindeer family," she said. "I can go the rest of the way back."

"When you or Francy need keys to the cabins, they are in a locked cabinet behind the registration desk. If I'm not around, Dad has an extra set in his room."

She nodded and hurried toward the lodge, thinking about Andy.

Andy does work for Orson and he doesn't have much to do with the lodge or his family.

Her focus turned to the website photo she had seen of him. He appeared to have an affluent lifestyle...or at least that was the impression he wanted to give.

Once inside her room, she sat down at the desk and turned on her computer. When she called a client, she put her cell on speaker and typed notes as she talked. Opening a new Word document, she titled it Voyageurs

Embezzlement/Murder Notes and called Orson's
office number first.

"Good morning, Voyageurs Financial Trust, this is
Myrtle," a pleasant voice answered.

"Good morning. Is Mr. Meade in today?"

"What time is your appointment?"

"My name is Lainey Maynard and I need to speak
with Mr. Meade today, please."

"I'm sorry. He only takes meetings by appointment.
If you would like to schedule a meeting, his first
opening is in February."

*February? Is she serious? What investment service is
booked up for two months?*

"Myrtle, I'm an investigator with…"

"Hold, please." The pleasant voice changed and was
clearly angered.

The line clicked and elevator music began playing.
Lainey was typing, noting Myrtle's change of attitude.
She watched the clock on her screen. Five minutes
passed before the annoying music stopped. The line
clicked once more.

"This is Orson Meade. Who in Hades are you? I've
not hired an investigator!"

"Sir, I'm Lainey Maynard. We've been hired to
investigate the embezzlement claim against Jake
Watson. I need to speak with you as soon as possible,
perhaps early this afternoon."

Meade was silent, but she could hear his raspy

breathing become more rapid. A few seconds passed before she spoke again.

"I am asking to meet with you this afternoon, Mr. Meade, to gather information. Would 1 p.m. at your office be convenient?"

He cleared his voice a couple of times and let out an audible sigh.

"If you insist, I'll clear my calendar for this afternoon at 1 p.m. I expect you to be prompt and bring proof of who you are and details of this preposterous claim." With that said, he hung up.

She finished her notes, trying to write the wording he had used about a 'preposterous' case.

"Meade, old boy, I don't scare easily." She said aloud. She reread through Snoops's notes mentioning that, according to Sadie, Orson had fired Jake and threatened to prosecute.

Lainey thought for a minute, then used the office phone to call Clyde.

"Already in trouble, are you?" the voice answered.

"Sounds like someone didn't get his coffee this morning," she teased.

"Coffee's fine. What have you found out?"

"I met briefly with Sadie Watson, and I think the documents she said were solid proof of her husband's innocence have been altered. Can I scan them to you for verification of my suspicions?"

"Of course. What else?"

"There is an excel spreadsheet showing client account numbers…and the dollar amount of this one file is more than $50,000,000."

Snoops paused briefly.

"Send that file, too. I'll see what I can find out. Have you talked with Voyageur's owner, Orson Meade?"

"How do you know about Meade? I didn't tell you!"

"I said I would check up on you."

She rolled her eyes. "I have a meeting with him this afternoon, but if our conversation a few minutes ago is any indication, he's going to be hostile."

"We need to step carefully, Lainey. If you're going to record the conversation, make sure you put the recorder on the desk so he is aware."

"Yes, sir. It's just that he might not open up with a recorder in front of his face."

"You're not a rookie. If we need this conversation as evidence, let's cover our bases, so it's not thrown out."

She took a breath and blew it out, loud enough she knew he heard it.

"Snoops, will you run a background on Andy McAndrews? He's an employee of Meade's and my gut tells me he may not be on the up-and-up."

"What information do you have about him?"

"Until I get to Meade's office, I only have the information listed on the company's website. Can you use any of that?"

"I'll try. What time is your meeting?"

"1 p.m."

"Have you contacted the local law enforcement office if you need a backup?"

"Not yet. I'll…" he cut her off in mid-sentence.

"You'll go by the police station after your meeting, right?"

She blew out another loud breath in protest.

"I mean it. Stop by and at least let them know who you are and what you're doing. You know you're going to need the police report of Jake Watson's death."

"I will go by there after my meeting." She knew he was right. She needed any information the police report or the autopsy report might contain.

"Good. Send me the files."

"Right away. Thank you."

"And Lainey," he added, sounding more like her father than her boss, "Go to the police station. Your safety is important."

"I promise. Talk with you soon."

"You'd better!"

She disconnected from the call and scanned in the pages, the spreadsheet, and the photo. Clyde Bedlow was the expert and she had confidence if anything was amiss, he could find it.

It was close to noon and Lainey changed clothes quickly and called Della's cell.

"How was your reindeer walk this morning?" Della inquired instead of answering with the standard 'hello'.

"You're too funny," she replied. "I need to use the Tahoe this afternoon. Are you in your room so I can come by and pick up the keys?"

"Sure. I'm here with Francy. We've found something that you might be interested in."

"I'll be right there."

She ended the call, grabbed her backpack and coat, making sure the recorder was snuggly in the pocket, and walked down the hall to the Monty Moose room. She knocked and Della quickly opened the door.

"I don't have much time, but what have you and Francy found?"

"Remember that picture I told you I didn't like? The one hanging in the bathroom?"

Lainey nodded and walked into the room.

"When I got back from breakfast, that picture was gone and hanging in its place was this." She handed her a framed 8 X 10 flyer. It listed the name of the hotel, how to call room service, and the checkout times.

"What?" Lainey asked, looking twice at the picture framed notice. "While we ate breakfast, someone broke into your room to trade out a photo for this flyer?"

"Exactly!" Francy added. "Look at the wall where the flyer hung."

Lainey walked into the bathroom and examined the wall. There was no mistake. A six-inch square on the wall had been patched. She put her hand on the area and felt the smooth finish on the square.

"That's a drywall patch!" she turned to look at her friends. "And the plaster is still damp."

"We waited to talk with you before telling Kevin or calling the police," Della said. "I think we should open it back up and see what's behind it."

"You know we can't do that," Francy stated. "We took pictures. I can send them to your phone, Lainey."

"Thanks. How long did we spend in the cafe for breakfast?"

"I checked with Shep. He thought about an hour or so."

"Does he know about this?"

"Not yet," Della added, "But he knows something is going on."

"If you think about it," Francy said cautiously, "Besides Jim, Kevin was the only person in the hotel that had a key to this room."

Lainey's mind raced. Jim couldn't get to the room, cut a hole in the wall, and patch in within an hour. Then her heart sank.

Kevin ate with us. When would he have time to do the switch? And why?

"Right now, I have to leave for a meeting in town with Meade," she blurted. "Don't mention the wall to anyone, not Vera or Shep or…" she paused. "…Kevin until I get back."

They agreed. Della handed her the Tahoe keys and Lainey left to drive to her appointment in town. The thought that Kevin had something to do with this had shaken her. She took a few deep breaths and gathered her thoughts as she drove to the office of Voyageurs Financial Trust.

The one-story office wasn't hard to find. A larger-than-life sign on the roof spread the entire distance of the building. Lainey parked the car and went inside, expecting to be greeted by Myrtle. Instead, the reception desk was vacant except for a small out-to-lunch sign with the request to ring the bell for assistance. The round silver bell was old and its ring was anything but loud. She hit the button a few times, but no one came.

She walked behind the desk and into a hallway that led to individual offices before she heard the front door open. She turned around to see a short, well-dressed, white-haired lady glaring at her.

"Can't you read the sign? It says ring the bell!"

"I rang the bell several times, and no one answered."

"Does that give you the right to wander through our office?" the lady took off her coat and walked behind the reception desk. "You're that investigator, aren't you?"

Lainey smiled, trying to ease the tension in the air.

"Yes, and you must be Myrtle. I apologize for not waiting longer. I didn't want to be late for my meeting with Mr. Meade."

The lady's disgust was apparent. She looked at

Lainey for a long minute before saying she would let Meade know his appointment had arrived.

"You wait here," she commanded. "I'll come get you when he is ready."

"Thank you."

Lainey watched her walk down the hallway and noticed she entered the first office without knocking on the door.

What receptionist goes into the boss's office when the door is closed without knocking or calling him first? I think little Miss Myrtle Meanie has more than a business relationship with good old Orson.

It wasn't long before Myrtle returned.

"He'll see you now. It's the first door on the right." She sat down and tried to look busy, ignoring Lainey completely.

"Thank you. Have a good day."

There was no response. She walked the short distance to the first office on the right. The door was standing open, but she knocked on the door frame anyway.

"Mr. Meade?" she asked. "It's Lainey Maynard. May I come in?"

The room wasn't large. An over-sized couch and ottoman made it appear even smaller. A fairly plain desk was centered in the room. Behind it was a bay window with potted plants that appeared to have died months ago. A man was sitting behind the desk, his chair turned with its back to the door.

Lainey blinked in surprise when he turned the chair around. It was Andy McAndrews, not Olson Meade. She quickly gathered her composure and walked over to pretend to greet him.

"It's nice to meet you, Mr. Meade," she said, holding out her hand to shake his.

The young man raised his eyebrows, smiled, then stood up.

"Hello, sweetheart. Aren't you an afternoon delight."

His toothy grin made Lainey's stomach turn over. He walked from behind the desk and, instead of shaking her hand, he kissed it.

Instantly, she jerked her hand away and walked backward a couple of steps.

"Now, now, just relax. I didn't mean anything." The Cheshire cat grin that spread across his entire face made her want to slap him silly.

"I'm not Orson Meade," he said, walking toward the office door. "I'm just filling in for him for a few minutes. Have a seat and I'll see if he's available." His arrogance was proof that her first impression of him from the website photo was accurate. He made her skin crawl.

She sat on the edge of the couch where she could see the hallway and anyone who walked by. Within a few minutes, a stocky, older man rushed through the doorway. The awkward way he spoke and the fact that his face was scarlet screamed out his discomfort with the meeting.

"I told you how busy I am," he said as he sat behind his desk. "What is it you want?"

Lainey stood up, walked over to the desk, and put her hand out.

"Thank you for meeting with me, Mr. Meade. It's nice to meet you."

He did not return the gesture. Instead, his eyes turned to the doorway. He got up quickly, walked over to the door, and closed it. As he walked back to his desk, he motioned for her to sit down.

"What's this about an investigation? I have done nothing wrong."

Lainey sat down slowly, and just as slowly, she took her notes from her backpack. She wanted to make him squirm. The more nervous he became, the more she had the upper hand. It was then she remember what Snoops had told her about the recorder. She put her hand inside her coat pocket and switched it on.

"Mr. Meade, I need to let you know that I'm here to investigate an embezzlement charge. I will record this meeting to provide…"

"Isn't that a coincidence? I'm recording this conversation, too."

So he records his meetings? That's an interesting fact to know.

"Several weeks ago, you accused Jake Watson, one of your employees, of embezzling money from your clients. Is that true?"

"I had been given information that he *might* have been. I never filed a formal complaint."

"What made you think he was stealing money?"

Orson took a deep breath and his face was returning to a natural, pale color.

"Jake was my most trusted employee. He was like a son to me. Over the past few years, an error might have appeared, but he assured me that's what it was. An error."

"I see. What made you finally confront him?"

"A client came to me with what she thought was proof that money had been stolen from her account. Since she was a valued client, I audited the account. After an exhausting search, I realized that someone had indeed been stealing money from her and blamed the losses on the volatile market conditions. The account manager was Jake."

"So you fired him."

"Yes, I had no choice but to let him go."

"And when he tried to tell you he was innocent, you threatened to prosecute him, correct?"

The man leaned forward in his chair. Fear was in his eyes.

"Who told you…" his voice got louder. "This is the

doings of that wife of his, isn't it? She's the only one who knew I said that."

Lainey waited to respond, hoping his fear would cause him to panic and give up more information. It did.

"Look, he was like a son to me. I was angry and hurt. Jake had told me many times before he needed a raise because his wife, Sadie, wanted things. Fancy things. Expensive cars and jewelry. He was afraid she would leave him if he didn't please her."

He leaned back in his chair and looked down at his hands for several seconds.

"When I was told about the missing money, the pieces seemed to fit. I knew Jake needed the money badly, and the audit showed he was guilty." His voice cracked. "Never did I think the boy would take his own life."

"I'm sorry to have upset you, Mr. Meade. I think, for now, that is all the questions I have." She stood up to leave. "Thank you, sir. I'll see myself out."

She walked to the door and opened it. She wasn't surprised to see Myrtle standing to the right of the door, just out of sight. Startled, the older lady looked away as if she hadn't seen Lainey and hurried toward the end of the hallway. She disappeared into the women's bathroom.

Lainey walked back through the reception area and

out to her car. Before starting the car, she pulled the recorder out of her pocket and spoke into it.

"Notes: Andy is a schmuck. Find out why Myrtle was listening outside the office door."

She flipped the off button, put the recorder back in her coat pocket. She took her cell phone to program in the directions to the police station.

Snoops was right. There is more to this case and the police should have information that could answer some of the questions I have.

CHAPTER 8

Within ten minutes, Lainey was standing outside the police station entrance staring at an intercom button. She pushed the buzzer and waited for someone to answer.

"Police station," the male voice responded. "How can I help you?"

"I'd like to speak with the Chief, please."

"What is your name?"

"Lainey Maynard. I'm an investigator."

"He's been expecting you. Please enter and sit down. There are chairs on the right side of the waiting room."

The door behind her clicked loudly. She opened it, and as instructed, she sat down in a chair in the small waiting area. The walls were a sterile white color and reminded her of a hospital corridor. She'd been in many police stations over the years and understood why their rooms were not warm and welcoming. No one comes to a station for a vacation.

Lainey's mind was replaying the statement by the dispatcher…'He's been expecting you.' She knew Snoops had alerted him and wasn't sure if she was glad or if she resented it.

She heard footsteps, and the only door in the room opened. Her mouth dropped open and the shock on her face betrayed her. She stood up quickly, dropping her backpack. When she bent over to pick it up, she stepped on the tail of her coat and fell forward, landing flat on her face directly in front of the officer.

"We stopped having people bow to us years ago," the chief grinned, putting out his hand to help her up. "It's good to see you, too."

"Sven Jorgensen? You're the Chief?" she asked, trying to hide her embarrassment.

"Guilty as charged. I've been the police chief for several years."

"Clyde Bedlow told you about me, didn't he?" she commented as she regained her composure. "Did you know who I was when we met at in the library parking lot?"

"Mr. Bedlow is very professional and thorough. He called concerning the case you are working on a few days ago."

"I see. How do you know Kevin McAndrews? I thought he called you the night of the parade."

"We've been friends a long time. He's a good guy."

"Why didn't you tell me who you were?"

"I was told to wait until you contacted me, but to keep an eye on you. Imagine my surprise when Kevin asked me to find a parking place for one of the guests helping out at the lodge. He told me your first name and that you'd be driving a Nebraska red Tahoe. Until you introduced yourself, I didn't make the connection."

"You didn't watch the parade, did you? You were watching me."

"Surveillance is one of my specialties. Let's move to my office where we can talk in more detail."

She nodded and walked through the doorway. He made sure the door was closed behind them.

"My office is the last one on the left," he said, leading the way.

He entered the office ahead of her, motioning for her to take a seat in one of the two chairs in front of a metal desk.

"Thank you," she said.

She put her backpack on the chair to the right and took out her computer. Then she laid her coat across the back of that chair and sat in the chair on the left. It was directly in front of Sven's chair.

The Chief sat down behind his desk and waited for her to get settled.

"I understand you are a coffee drinker," he stated. "I

believe your drink of choice is a skinny Mocha Frappe."

Lainey rolled her eyes. "When Clyde gives details, he sometimes goes overboard."

"We tend to drink coffee at the station, too. Did you notice the coffee shop across the street? We're regulars…and we get coffee free." He laughed. "Would you like a frappe?"

"That would be great," she smiled.

He's trying to butter you up, Lainey. Be nice, but don't let your guard down.

He picked up the phone on his desk, hit a preset button, and a number dialed instantly.

"Morning. This is Chief Jorgensen. I need a skinny Mocha Frappe and my regular. Terry will be over in a few minutes. Thanks."

He hung up the receiver, looked in his top desk drawer and pulled out a file folder, but did not open it immediately.

"Mr. Bedlow gave me a few of the details of this case they assigned you. However, he said you would fill me in. I'm listening."

"Sadie Watson hired my company to investigate the charges of embezzlement that Voyageurs' CEO, Orson Meade, made against her husband, Jake. She claimed to have proof of his innocence and knew he'd been framed."

Her computer was open and running and for a

second, she thought about taking the recorder out of her coat pocket and either playing the records to him or recording her conversation with him. But she decided against that for the moment. She needed to find out what information the police had first.

"And what did you find out when you met with Mrs. Watson last evening?"

Lainey shrugged her shoulders and let out a long breath.

"She was late and very nervous. I believe she felt that someone was watching or following her, but I have no proof of that. She gave me an envelope that contained, according to her, proof of Jake's innocence."

Sven tapped his fingers on the file folder in front of him. She could tell he was deciding whether or not to share the file with her.

"You sound suspicious of that information. Do you doubt its authenticity?"

"I feel the invoices were altered. Logos and font are slightly different from on the website. I've sent them to the office to verify my suspicions."

The chief raised his right hand and rubbed his chin. The straight line that his thin lips made across his face told Lainey he was withholding information. She didn't want to lay all of her cards on the table at the moment, either. She continued to question him cautiously.

"Were you aware of the embezzlement charge prior to getting the call about Jake's death?"

"Not at that time. Dispatch received a 911 call from his wife. She said he had shot himself."

"Wait...Sadie said he had committed suicide? Not that he had been shot?"

The officer nodded. "All 911 calls are recorded. She said he shot himself."

"Things aren't adding up here. Can I see a copy of the police or coroner's report?"

He opened the file and handed her a document.

"This is the coroner's findings. Cause of death was a self-inflicted gunshot wound to the head."

Lainey took the report and looked at it closely. She looked up to speak when the officer handed her another set of papers with photos clipped to them.

"Here is the police report from that night. Attached are photos of the scene. I hope you're not squeamish. Some of these are graphic."

At that moment, there was a knock on his office door.

"It's Terry, sir. I've got your coffee."

Sven walked over to the door, opened it, took the coffee, and thanked the young officer. He closed the door and walked over to hand the frappe to Lainey. Her face had turned pale, and he knew the pictures had upset her.

She put down the papers and photos and took the coffee.

"Thanks," she said, taking a sip, hoping to clear her mind of the images she had just seen.

The chief walked back to his desk and sat down. He took several sips from his steaming cup, giving her time to regroup her thoughts.

"Did the officers who responded to the call think anything looked suspicious? I mean, did they question whether Jake shot himself?"

"Anytime there is a suspected suicide, we investigate it as if it were a homicide until the time that it is proven to be a suicide. It was Jake's gun. His finger prints were the only ones on it and the coroner found powder residue on his fingers."

Lainey was quiet, thinking about Sadie's claims, the tampered evidence, and why she mentioned murder.

"I'd like you to look at the information Sadie Watson gave me last night." She took the envelope out of her backpack to hand to Sven.

"I've seen the papers. Clyde emailed them to me before you arrived. He verified they are not original documents." He paused, taking a drink of his coffee. "The man in the photo is Andrew McAndrews, Kevin's brother."

She put the envelope back in the backpack. "I met him by accident this morning at Meade's office."

"What was your impression of him?"

"Arrogant, sleazy, a wolf in sheep's clothing..." she grimaced. "Need I go on?"

"Nope. That's a fairly accurate description."

"I've been hired to investigate whether the embezzlement charge against Jake was bogus. Was he set up? Or did he take the money and couldn't handle the guilt?"

"Unless you have proof that will stand up in court showing someone set him up, I can't open an investigation. Meade did not file any lawsuit or formal complaint with our office."

"Do you have any background information on Sadie or Andy McAndrews? Anything that might help me going forward?"

"Neither have a criminal record," he began. "Andy had a few speeding tickets and been involved in a couple of fender benders in his younger days."

"I understand. Sadie is hiding something, and I not going to give up on finding out what that is. Thank you for meeting with me." She stood, slipped on her coat, and picked up the backpack.

Sven stood, walking from the desk to open the office door for her.

"You need to keep in touch with me," he said. "That's an order from your main office guy, Mr. Bedlow."

"And if you find out anything that might help me, will you contact me?"

"If I can."

"Thanks." She started to walk out the door, paused and then turned back to face the chief.

"I didn't get a chance to thank you for helping me avoid the parade traffic last evening. I really appreciate it."

"You're welcome. Say hello to Kevin for me."

She nodded. "I'll do that!"

Lainey's mind was preoccupied, processing and reviewing the information she received. The drive back to Reindeer Lodge seemed to take no time all. She pulled the Tahoe into the parking lot, took out her backpack, and walked into the lobby. She didn't get far into the lodge before she stopped in her tracks. Kevin and his brother were arguing loudly in the middle of the room.

"I've told you before not to come here and upset Dad," Kevin said angrily. "He doesn't need to deal with you ever again!"

"That's a laugh," Andy, replied smugly. "He would have lost this rotten old lodge years ago if I hadn't jumped in to save it."

"Save it? You? Don't deny that since Mom died, you've done everything in your power to force him to sell it."

"And what, dear little brother, have you done? Clean out stables, paint the walls," Andy spouted. He pointed around the room. "Of course your stupid

Christmas decorations have been bringing in tons of paying customers!"

Shep and Vera heard the voices from the hallway and were standing just behind the registration desk, watching and listening. They looked at Lainey and then back at the two men.

"Get out of here before my anger gets the best of me and I throw you out."

Andy laughed loudly. "You really want your name in the paper again for assault?" He walked closer to his younger brother. "Go ahead. You're used to letting your fists fight your battles instead of your brain."

The air was thick with tension and the seconds felt like hours. Kevin's face was red. He was grinding his teeth, hard. As quick as a professionally trained boxer, he threw a punch that landed squarely in the middle of Andy's face. He fell to the floor like a tons of bricks.

"If you come back to this lodge, it'll be the last thing you ever do," Kevin sneered. "You are not welcome here."

He walked away, leaving his brother lying on the floor.

Shep, waiting until he was sure Kevin had gone outside, walked over to help Andy up. He put out his hand, but the hurt man ignored it.

"Thanks, but I don't need help," he snorted, getting up by himself. "Here's a word of advice…check out of this place before he comes after you."

Lainey watched as Andy walked past her toward the door. He stopped long enough to speak to her.

"If you have the hots for that, you're not my type anyway." He scowled and left the lodge.

"Why did he say that to you?" Vera asked. "My gosh, what's going on here?"

"I ran into him at Voyageur's. The bigger question is what were these two arguing about?"

"Jim told me that Andy brought foreclosure papers and pressured him to sign them. It upset him and Kevin," Shep answered. "The boys have been at odds for years."

Della and Francy had been standing on the top of the stairs, seeing only the punch and hearing Kevin's threats.

"Who was that? Why did Kevin punch him?" Francy asked.

Lainey headed up the stairs before answering.

"That was Kevin's brother, Andy."

"I saw him a few minutes ago coming out of Jim's room," Della said. "He didn't seem upset. In fact, he was smiling."

"Shep, do you think Jim feels up to me asking him a few questions?" Lainey asked. "I'd like to know more about Kevin."

"You mean you want to know more about the assault Andy mentioned," Vera added. "I do too. Let's go see him!"

"Now wait a minute," Shep replied. "Jim doesn't need another round of twenty-questions at the moment. Let me talk with him first."

Lainey nodded. "You're right. I'm sure this hasn't been easy for him."

"Don't you all have chores you are supposed to be handling?" he said, trying to change the subject. "Remember, we only have a few days before the next guests arrive."

"Right, again. Let me put my things in my room and change clothes."

"And we have things to talk about," Francy reminded. "We still need to…meet in Della's room to talk about our game plan going forward." She looked at Lainey, then at Della. Her eyes opened wide as if she was giving a secret code.

"Yes, we have things to discuss!" Della answered. "I'll meet you two in my room, say fifteen minutes?"

"Sounds good." Lainey said and walked quickly to her room. In less than ten minutes, she was knocking on Della's door.

"Come in," Francy called out, "the door is open."

Lainey walked in and was surprised to see Vera standing with her hands on her hips, facing her two friends. She appeared to be scolding them as if they were children again.

"You sit down, too, young lady," Vera commanded.

"I want to know why you didn't tell me about the bathroom wall!"

"Mom," Francy began impatiently, "We didn't want to worry you and Lainey said..."

"That's a bunch of hooey! I've helped you many times. I've been a cat burglar, cooked stink bait that made my hands smell for days, and my backside has been in the newspaper. You could say I'm famous!"

The three ladies laughed loudly.

"You're certainly famous, alright," Della grinned. "You and Shep mooned someone! No one knew whose derrieres were in that photo."

"Nonetheless, I'm going to help."

"Vera, I don't know what we would do without you," Lainey chuckled.

"And don't any of you forget that! Now, what's with the patch on the wall?"

Della explained how, after breakfast, she discovered that the first photo was changed out for the current flyer that hung on the wall. When she took down the flyer to look more closely, she found the patched area.

"Did you look behind the first photo, the one you thought was watching you?" Vera asked. "Could the patch have been there before the switch was made?"

"She didn't, but the putty was still sticky this morning when we touched it. That tells me it was a recent repair," Francy stated.

"I think we need to talk with Kevin about this,"

Della remarked. "He's the handyman and should know if there had been a repair made and why the picture was taken down."

"After the confrontation he had with his brother, maybe we should let him cool off a bit," Lainey said. "It's getting dark and I still need to work on the Watson case."

"Shep baked tater tot chicken hot dish casserole for supper. It should be ready by now," Vera smiled. "He likes to serve it while it's hot."

"Great. I hope he has more cornbread and honey from last night."

The group headed down the stairs to Bella's Cafe. The lobby was eerily quiet and each of them felt an uneasiness thinking about the confrontation between the brothers an hour earlier. The smell of fresh baked bread filled the hallway leading to the cafe door. Jim greeted them, sitting not in his wheelchair, but at a regular table.

"We've been expecting you! Smell that great sourdough bread? Sit down with me. Shep will be right out with our dinner."

"I love homemade sourdough! Wonder if he made cinnamon butter?" Della took a deep breath in and let it out slowly.

"He made honey-butter with our local honey."

"Good to see you in a regular chair, Jim," Lainey commented. "You feeling a little better?"

"Doctors said it would be a slow recovery, but at the moment, I'm happy to be sharing this table with you all." He shrugged and his eyes became teary. "I understand you witnessed my boys arguing this afternoon." He looked down at the table and swallowed hard.

"We understand," Lainey tried to comfort him and touched his shoulder lightly. "We've all had spats with family."

"My boys," he sighed. "My boys don't have spats. They have knock-down drag-out wars with each other. It's been worse since their mother died. She was better at keeping the peace between them than I am."

"Enough small talk," Shep said as he walked from the kitchen to their table. "It's time to fill your plates with Chick Chick Hot Dish," he joked. "It's a new recipe I'm testing on you tonight!"

"Catchy name! Sounds almost sinful!" Francy said. "I am hungry!"

The mood at the table lightened, and the conversation shifted to memories about the two's army buddy days and their adventures as young soldiers. As the food was passed around for the third time, each person raved about the chef and his new creation.

"You can test your recipes on me anytime, my friend," Jim said as he put down his fork. "I'm so full, you're going to need that wheelchair to roll me back to my room!"

"You got it!" Shep laughed. "I'm happy to!"

"Sweetie, why don't you take Jim back to his room while the girls and I clean up," Vera said. "It's the least we can do to thank you for dinner."

"After all," Della added, "We are the Whoopee Merry Maids Service, you know!"

"You ladies are the best," Jim smiled. "I'm so thankful you are here!"

Shep helped Jim into the wheelchair and took back to his room. Within an hour, the ladies had finished cleaning up the kitchen and were back in their own rooms for the night.

CHAPTER 9

L ainey hadn't been in her room more than a few minutes when her cell phone rang.

"Someone's been in my room again...and this time, they left the hole in the wall open." Della almost shouted into the phone.

"Touch nothing. I'll be right there."

She ended the call, left her room and ran down the hallway. Della's door was open and Francy was already there, looking at the hole in the bathroom wall.

"Whatever was there, is gone now." Francy turned to Lainey. "Della needs to stay in my room until we find out what's going on. Don't you agree?"

"Absolutely. Was anything of yours taken, Della? Or was anything out of place?"

"None of my things were taken. The wall plaster debris on the bathroom floor is the only thing I saw."

Shep and Vera walked through Della's door at that moment. He was clearly not happy.

"Vera filled me in and I'm upset that you didn't feel you could tell me this morning."

He looked around the bathroom and then turned back to the ladies. He was not smiling.

"What if Della had been in this room? What if she had been sleeping and…" He shook his head as his voice trailed off.

"I'm the one who said not to involve you. I wanted time to speak with Kevin before we accused him or anybody of anything," Lainey confessed.

"Jim mentioned to me that when Kevin is upset, he goes to a small pub in the area and plays pool all night. It's his outlet. So I doubt he's here tonight. But we," he looked at Lainey, "And I mean *we* will talk to him first thing in the morning."

"I agree, too," Vera chimed in. "We will talk to Kevin together."

"No, Vera, you will not talk to Kevin. Lainey and I will handle this. We don't want to *confront* him. We only want to *talk* with him."

"Humph," Vera crossed her arms in protest. "I can see when I not wanted!" She stomped out of the room and down the hallway.

Francy rolled her eyes. "Don't worry about Mom. I'll talk to her. By the time she gets to her room, she'll realize Shep was right."

"I'll get my things together and move to your room, Francy," Della said. She took her suitcase out of the closet and placed in on the bed. "It won't take me a minute to pack."

"Sounds good. I'll feel better once we are out of this room."

"Lainey and I are going to let you pack," Shep said, motioning for her to leave with him. "I'll see you both at breakfast."

"Thank you," Della replied, as she walked over to give him a hug. "I hope Vera's happier once you get to your room."

"When it comes to her or your safety..." he said slyly. "Her favorite saying applies to her, too."

"And which saying is that?"

He grinned. "You can get happy in the same pants you got mad in."

"You can say that again!" Francy laughed. "I've heard her say that a million times!"

Shep and Lainey walked out and turned toward the Andy Antelope room where she was staying. "Let's talk a minute about our strategy for tomorrow morning," Shep said as Lainey unlocked the door. The two walked inside. He stood by the door and she sat on the edge of the bed.

"Don't be upset with the others," Lainey said to apologize once more. "I did not want to involve you."

He nodded, and his face softened a little.

"After we talk with Kevin, we will decide whether
or not to call the police in on this."

Shep explained that when Vera told him about the
bathroom wall incident, he asked Jim, who had keys to
the rooms in the lodge, to use the keys. He used the
excuse of needing to clean the rooms, not letting on
that anything else was wrong.

"Jim said the only people with master keys were
himself, Kevin, and me."

Lainey stood up and paced around the small room.
Walking or moving helped her sort out her thoughts.
She stopped to face her friend.

"I can't believe Kevin has anything to do with this.
He could come into these rooms at any time. Why
would he wait till now? Why wait till we are here and
risk suspicion? What is he hiding?"

"Those are good questions that we need to ask him.
When he comes for breakfast, ask him to meet with us
before he goes to work. He won't feel defensive if you
approach him that way."

"I will do that. I will plan on meeting you in the cafe
at 6 a.m."

"That will work. It's been a long day for all of us.
Try to get some rest and let's start fresh in the
morning."

She smiled and nodded. Shep smiled, waved, and
walked out of her room. She locked the door behind

him. Instantly, as if a timer had gone off, her cell phone rang.

"What has happened now?" she muttered out loud. Pulling her cell phone from her pocket, she answered quickly. It was Snoops.

"Hey, boss. You're working late, aren't you?"

"Checking up on you can be a never-ending job."

"Someone has to keep you on your toes!" she chuckled.

"Finally met Sven, did you?"

"You know I did. Thanks for sharing that a Mocha Frappe is the way to soften me up!"

"I thought you'd appreciate that."

"Sure...and the fact that you shared with him the Sadie information I gave you before you told me they had been tampered with. Yeah...I really appreciated that. Does making me look inept give you pleasure?"

There was a brief moment of silence on the phone. Lainey's cheeks felt hot and her voice had raised a pitch or two. She took a couple of breaths to calm down.

"I intended to let you know first, but the timing didn't work out to do that. I didn't share everything with him, if that is any consolation to you."

"Depends on what it is you didn't share," she answered flatly, trying to sound as if she didn't care. The truth was, she cared...a lot.

"Jake told his father, Louis, that he thought Sadie was cheating on him. He said he was depressed and didn't know where to turn. Louis hired a private investigator several months ago to follow her."

"That's why she was nervous when I met her. She knew she was being watched!"

There was another pause in the conversation. It was as if a light bulb had flashed brightly in Lainey's eyes, then dimmed just as quickly.

"But why would this P.I. still be following her after Jake's death?" she asked.

"That's the definitive question of the day. Why, indeed."

"Do you know the name of this person?"

The was a slight grunt from Snoops. She giggled to herself.

Two can play this game, my friend. I still know how to push your buttons, just like you know how to push mine!

"Of course I have his name."

"And that name would be?"

"Pierce Knight. He's based out of Florida and has a reputation for being the best around."

"Sounds like Louis Watson spared no expense when hiring him. Florida to Minnesota is not the average daily commute."

"I've emailed you his contact information."

"Thanks. I'll get on that. Anything else?"

"What did you find out from Orson Meade?"

"He wasn't the most cooperative at first, but he

seemed sorry about Jake's death. Did you know that he never filed a formal complaint against him?"

"Yes, I did. And I have something I think you will find interesting."

"About Meade?"

"About Andy McAndrews. I understand you met him at Meade's office today."

Great. So Sven is one of your sources, too.

"Chief Jorgensen told you that."

"He shared that Andy did not leave a good impression on you."

"He's not a nice person, that's all I will say. What information do you have about him?"

"The agent number on the excel spreadsheet Sadie gave you," he waited to see if she would interrupt him. She didn't.

"It's a page from Andy's ledgers. It's his agent number…and it had not been tampered with."

Lainey's mind raced with ideas. She took a moment to sort them quickly.

"Do you know if the accounts listed had money stolen from them?" she asked, knowing he most likely didn't.

"I can't verify that without getting a search warrant for the records."

"And we can't justify asking for that without sufficient proof, correct?"

"Yes. Since no formal charges were filed, we do need substantial proof."

"Sadie seems to be the key here. I'll text her for another meeting."

"She called the office earlier today and wanted an update on the investigation."

"Really. Did you speak with her?"

"I was in a meeting when she left me a message. It appears she doesn't think you're doing such a wonderful job."

"That doesn't bother me. Did she give any other contact information other than the number I have?"

"No. But she did request that we contact her before noon tomorrow."

"I'll take care of that."

"She's not been honest with us, as you know. I can't prove that she is the one who altered those invoices or how she got a copy of Andrew's ledger page. But I'm convinced she's trying to accuse Andy of embezzling the money."

"It looks that way, doesn't it? I'll put some pressure on her when I speak with her."

"One more item, Lainey. Sven is going to be watching you. You won't always see him, but if you need him, call him."

"But I…"

"Argue all you want. I'm concerned about where

this investigation is leading. You have no say in this. He will watch out for you and update me."

She knew Snoops was trying to keep her safe. She sighed and replied.

"I understand. There is more to this than embezzlement. And I'll keep him in the loop."

"And you'll keep me in the loop."

"I think you own the loop! You know things before they happen."

"That's why I'm Clyde Bedlow, alias Snoops!"

"You've earned that title."

"Check in with me tomorrow evening. I want an update on your talk with Sadie and what you find out about Pierce Knight. Do yourself a favor and get some rest tonight. My gut tells me you're going to have a long day tomorrow."

"Will do. Talk with you later."

She ended the call and plugged in the phone to charge it. She shook her head, admiring the intelligence and intuition of her friend. He was right, she was tired. Tomorrow would be a long day. As if talking with Sadie and finding Pierce Knight wouldn't make for a full day, she still had to talk with Kevin and clean two cabins!

Lainey took a shower and got ready to hit the sack. Falling asleep would be another issue. She texted a note to herself to ask Della or Francy to help with her assigned cleaning duties in case she didn't have time.

She turned off the lights, closed her eyes, and tried to fall asleep.

The phone alarm blasted, jolting her awake. She fumbled to hit the stop button, and the time read 5 a.m. Stretching and rubbing her eyes, she felt like she had just fallen asleep. Walking clumsily to the bathroom to splash water on her face, she stubbed her little toe on the doorstop.

"Ouch!" she cried loudly, hobbling over to the side of the bathtub to sit down. She rubbed the toe and grimaced. "This hurts worse than hitting your elbow!"

The throbbing finally stopped and before long, she had dressed and was ready to walk down to Bella's cafe. She picked up her backpack, locked the door, and thought about what she would say to Kevin at breakfast.

To her surprise, her friends and Jim were already sitting at a table, chowing down on biscuits and gravy. She looked at her watch. It wasn't even 6 a.m. She thought she was early.

"Look who decided to wake up this morning!" Francy teased. "We were about to call the National Guard out to find you."

"Very funny. You guys are early!"

"They are," Shep replied. "My little sweetheart was still a bit upset this morning and got up earlier than usual."

"And when his little sweetheart is up early, she makes sure everyone is up." Della kidded.

"I'm ignoring you all," Vera said, trying to sound smug. "Maybe I was a little loud walking down the hallway this morning."

"A little loud?" Francy questioned. "Playing the Star Spangled Banner on your cell phone speaker and singing the words…no, shouting the words, is more than a little loud!"

"And don't forget the 'accidental' knocking on our door," Della added. "As if she were confused about which room it was!"

"I apologized for that," Vera stated, sounding not apologetic at all. "I must have gotten turned around in the hall. I thought I was knocking on my door and Shep wasn't answering."

Jim tried not to smile or laugh while he listened to the conversation, but lost control when he heard her last excuse.

"Holy cow. I haven't laughed this hard in months! Vera, you're something special!" His belly laugh was contagious, causing everyone to join in.

"I've been telling these hyenas that for years!" She grinned.

"Gosh. How did I not hear that commotion? I'm usually a light sleeper," Lainey said as she sat down.

"No worries. Have breakfast. We've got cleaning to do today." Francy replied.

"That reminds me, would you or Della have time to help me with the two cabins I'm to clean? I'm sorry, but I have several things on my plate for work, and I'm not sure if they will take all day or not."

"I was going with Francy this morning to look at the cabins she needs to clean. We can certainly look at the other two when we've finished."

"Thank you. I'll let you know before noon if I need you."

Lainey watched the door for Kevin to enter, dreading the conversation that would follow. But he never came. An hour passed, still no Kevin. The group finished eating, had cleared away the dishes, and left to start on their assigned chores.

Shep sat down beside Lainey. He had a worried expression on his face.

"It's odd that Kevin isn't here," he said quietly. "Wonder if he's hung over or something?"

"I wondered the same thing. Think I'll walk down to the Snowy Woods and Caribou cabins to see how much cleaning needs to be done. Maybe he'll be at the lodge when I return."

"I'll watch for him and call you if he comes in."

"Thanks. I'll grab the spare keys and head out. Talk with you later."

She left the cafe, took the spare keys, and hurried down the path to the cabins. When she saw the wooden fork sign, her thoughts turned to Kevin. He had been so nice and when they visited the reindeer stalls, she saw compassion and caring in him. Where was he? What history of assault had Andy been referring to?

Following the path to the left, she passed the Snowy Woods cabin, thinking to start at the Caribou cabin since it was the farthest out. She would catch the other cabin on her way back to the lodge.

The log cabin had Christmas lights outlining the roof. She stepped onto what once had been a sculpted rock sidewalk leading from the main path to the cabin's front door. The ice blanket over it couldn't hide the cracked and aging stones. Years of harsh winters had taken their toll.

The small porch had four wide steps, with logs for handrails. She glanced at the reindeer shaped sign saying 'Caribou Cabin' but her attention quickly turned to the wooden front door. It was slightly ajar.

She stopped at the bottom of the steps, looking carefully around her. Not wanting to make a noise, she slowly walked around the cabin. The front door was the only way in or out. The two windows were too small and too far off the ground for an adult to climb through.

Facing the front door again, she pulled out her cell phone. She had saved Sven's cell phone number and pulled it up. All she had to do was hit the green 'dial' button and be connected.

Slowly, she walked up the steps and to the door. She

opened it wide enough to slip inside. The cabin was one big room. The only light was filtered gray rays coming from the two small windows. What she saw caused her to drop her phone in shock.

In the middle of the room stood Kevin, his back facing the door. When he heard her phone hit the floor, he spun half-way around. His face was pure white and his eyes were the size of half dollars. He looked at Lainey, then down at the floor, then at his right hand.

"Oh my Lord," she gasped. "What happened?"

Kevin didn't speak. He shook his head back and forth. Not taking her eyes off him, Lainey slowly bent down, picked up her phone and hit the dial button.

He didn't move or speak. It was as if he was frozen in place. He kept staring at his hand, then to the floor, then back at his hand in disbelief.

Lainey didn't move either. When she heard the police chef's voice answer, she did her best to speak, but her words kept getting caught in her throat.

"Get to Caribou cabin now. Something's terribly wrong. Kevin's here…he's holding a gun…and Andy's lying on the floor."

She watched the man closely, ready to run if he turned angry or approached her. She didn't know if he could hear how loudly her heart was pounding or if he sensed fear. Thoughts of her training, how to calm an armed intruder, how to protect herself from an attack, and how to not let fear take control, crowded in her mind.

The two stood in the cabin for what seemed like an eternity. Neither one moving nor speaking. Lainey never took her eyes off Kevin or the gun he gripped tightly in his hand. She heard footsteps running up the stairs, and still her eyes never moved. She felt the fast breathing of the police chief before she felt his hand on her shoulder.

"Lainey," he whispered in her ear. "When I talk to him, slowly back out the door. Officer Terry is waiting on the path. Don't nod or speak. Just do what I say."

Sven took his hand from her shoulder and stepped in front of her. Kevin had seen him. He was still holding the gun...and still not moving.

"Kev, buddy, it's me, Sven."

He waited for his friend to respond, but there was no answer. Lainey took a step backward.

"I'm here to help. You need to put the gun down first."

Kevin turned toward Sven, his eyes only a blank stare. He said nothing. Lainey took another step toward the door.

"It's okay. I'm your friend, remember? Put the gun down, buddy." Sven inched closer to him. Lainey took two steps backward and once she felt the threshold under her feet, turned and walked quickly down the steps. Officer Terry was there waiting for her.

"Get behind me," the officer said. "We've got an ambulance coming. I'm not leaving the Chief. When you see the EMT's close to the cabin, head to my patrol car. Stay there until I come get you."

She stood motionless, watching from the open doorway as Sven moved slowly toward Kevin. She strained to hear what was being said.

"I don't know what happened, but I'm going to help you. Put the gun down." Sven kept repeating to Kevin.

Suddenly, Kevin broke down and began sobbing uncontrollably. He dropped the gun and put his hands over his face. Sven moved quickly, grabbing hold of his buddy's hands. He yanked the handcuffs from his duty belt and had them around Kevin's hands in seconds. The chief shouted to the officer outside.

"Terry, it's clear. Is the ambulance here? I'm bringing him out. The gun's on the floor."

CHAPTER 10

Lainey watched as the chief walked Kevin down the path toward his patrol car. The EMT's arrived and were hurrying past her to get inside the cabin. Officer Terry called for backups and then turned his attention to her.

"Are you okay?"

She nodded.

"We're going to need a statement from you," he said. "For now, I'll walk you to the lodge."

"I understand. I can't believe Kevin would shoot his own brother."

The officer took her arm, and they walked down the path. Neither spoke until they were in the parking lot area. Two more patrol cars had arrived, and the Chief was talking with the officers. Kevin sat in the back of a patrol car, his head bent down.

Sven glanced at Lainey and motioned for her to wait for him to finish talking with his officers. Then he walked toward her.

"I'm glad you had my number, and you that weren't injured," he said in a reprimanding tone. "This is why I've been watching you so closely. I need you to tell me exactly what happened this morning."

"I know Kevin wouldn't shoot Andy," she mumbled.

"Why were you at the Caribou this morning?"

"Jim needed help cleaning the cabins. Caribou is one that I agreed to spruce up. Since I have the case I'm working on and needed to be in town this morning, I went to the cabin to see how much time I would need to get it cleaned for guests."

"What did you see when you got to the cabin?"

Lainey's gaze turned away from the chief to look again at the man sitting in the backseat of the patrol car. She swallowed and looked back to Sven.

"The door was open when I got to the cabin. I didn't know if it had been left open or if someone was inside. I walked around the cabin and saw no one or any signs of a break in."

"Did you hear the two talking or arguing inside the cabin?"

"No. I heard nothing. I went up the stairs and that's when I saw Kevin."

"What was he doing?"

"His back was to the door. He was standing over Andy, holding the gun in his right hand."

"When you walked up to the cabin, did you hear anything that sounded like a gunshot?"

"No. I was thinking about the phone calls I needed to make, but I would have known if someone had fired a gun."

The chief nodded, then looked at Kevin. His head still bowed. He hadn't moved or looked up since being put in the backseat.

"You need to come to the station and give a formal statement. Can you do that this morning?" he said. It was more like a command than a question.

She nodded she would.

"Is there anything you haven't told me? Anything between Andy and Kevin that I'm not aware of?"

She blinked. Her thoughts turned to the wall in Della's bathroom. She pursed her lips slightly, and the chief noticed.

"There is something you've not told me," he grimaced. "Get your facts together and meet me at the station in one hour…" he paused. "If you want to help Kevin, bring everything you have."

He turned, walked back to his patrol car, and got inside. She watched as he drove off. Officers were standing close by as the EMTs loaded Andy's body into the ambulance. Yellow police tape now blocked the path toward the cabins. She turned toward the lodge and saw Francy, Della, and Vera watching. She sighed and walked over to her friends.

"Does Jim know what happened?" Lainey asked the group.

"Shep is with him," Vera replied sadly. "He's in shock."

"Did you see Kevin shoot Andy?" Della asked. "I still can't believe this is happening."

"I didn't see who shot him. When I got to the cabin, Kevin was standing over the body."

Francy shook her head. "This looks bad, especially after the altercation those two had yesterday."

"In my heart, I don't see how he could shoot anyone," Lainey answered. "There are too many unanswered questions."

"What are we going to do?" Vera asked.

"We're going down to the police station and tell Chief Jorgensen about Della's bathroom wall and about the argument between the boys."

"We all need to go?" Della questioned.

"Yes, if we want to help Kevin…and Jim."

They nodded in agreement.

"Della, have you cleaned up the floor in your bathroom?"

"Not yet. Why?"

"Can you put those sheet rock pieces into a baggie to take to the station? Bring the framed flyer, too."

"You got it."

"Francy, will you call Shep and ask him to come down? He's going to need to give a statement, too."

"No need to call me. I'm here." He said as he walked toward them. "This hit Jim hard. He wants me to drive him to the station to see Kevin."

"Let's get our things together and meet back in the lobby in twenty minutes. We will go to the station together." She looked at Shep. "Will that give you time to get Jim ready and lock up the lodge?"

"He's waiting for me to get the car. I'll let him know we are all going."

The group walked back into the lodge and up the stairs to their rooms. Lainey's stomach was in knots. She called Snoops the second she got into her room.

"The police have arrested Kevin for his brother's murder? Is that what you said?"

"Yes. I know he didn't shoot Andy."

"This is a police matter now. What do you want me to do?"

"That spreadsheet of Andy's accounts that Sadie gave me, now that this is a murder investigation, can we get a search warrant for those records and the invoices that were tampered with?"

"I can get that done. You think Sadie is involved in this somehow?"

"How can she not be? After all, she's the one that accused Andy of embezzlement."

"Allegedly accused Andy," Snoops added. "Have you

called her this morning? The news of the shooting shouldn't be out yet. Try to reach her before she hears."

"I will. Can we subpoena Orson Meade and his receptionist, Myrtle?"

"Hold on…let's get the records first."

"Right. I'll let you know what I find out from Sadie."

"Don't forget about Pierce Knight, the private investigator Mr. Watson hired."

"He's next on my list to call."

Clyde hesitated before he spoke.

"My sources tell me Pierce Knight is in Minnesota. He's at the Best Western Hotel in Ranier."

"What? That can't be a coincidence. Ranier is only four miles from this lodge."

"Tell the chief, Lainey. Don't go to the hotel. We don't have any proof of anything, and if Pierce is involved, you don't want to scare him away."

She gave a soft growl in protest.

"I'll find out first."

"And you will tell Sven. If you don't, I will."

"Okay, okay. But not till I've spoken with Sadie. How long before I can get the records from Meade's office?"

"Most likely this afternoon. I'll email you."

"Thank you. I need to head to the police station."

She disconnected the call and immediately called the only number she had for Sadie Watson. The phone rang twice and went to voice mail. She left a message, trying to sound positive, but urgent.

"This is Lainey Maynard. I'm contacting you about your case and have important updates to share with you. Please call this number immediately. Thank you."

She ended that call and held down the home button on her phone. Her European male Siri voice asked, "Good morning Lainey. How can I help you?"

"Siri, call the phone number for the Best Western in Ranier, MN."

"Calling now."

The line rang four or five times before someone picked it up.

"It's Christmas at Ranier Best Western. Do you have a reservation?" The female sounded young and innocent.

"Do you have any rooms available for tonight?"

"We're booked, but I can take your name and call if we have a cancellation."

"No, thank you. I'll try another place."

"Ma'am, most of Ranier's hotels are booked solid for the season, but I know of a VRBO that might be available. It's a Vacation Rental By Owner. Would you like the contact information?"

"Yes, that would be great."

"It's called The Curious Moose. The owner's name is Andy and here is the phone number."

"Did you say Andy?" she questioned.

"Yes, Andy McAndrews. He's friends with my cousin. Did you get the number?"

"Sorry, no. Would you repeat it?" Stunned, she typed the number in her phone and emailed it herself.

"Thank you. That's a big help."

"You are welcome and Merry Christmas!"

Lainey put her phone in her backpack along with the papers Snoops had provided. She locked her room and walked to the lobby. Her thoughts were a jigsaw puzzle of pieces of information that she was desperately trying to fit together.

The group met in the lobby, then went to their cars to travel to the police station. Shep drove Vera and Jim in his truck. Lainey drove the Tahoe with Francy and Della. The ladies were quiet on the ride, each deep in thought. It wasn't until they parked the car at the station that Lainey spoke.

"Can the two of you do something for me this afternoon?"

Francy and Della looked at each other before answering.

"I thought we had to give the chief all of our information? Do you know something that you aren't going to share?" Francy, seated in the back seat, leaned forward and asked.

"Shortly before we left the lodge, I found information that may be crucial to the embezzlement investigation. I need proof that it is important, and I hoped you guys…"

"Of course we will," Della interrupted. "Tell us what you need."

Lainey briefly explained that Andy was the owner of a vacation rental home called The Curious Moose and she needed them to pretend to get a reservation that afternoon.

"You want us to go to this house and get what information?" Francy asked.

"I have a phone number to call, but I think you should go there. See if you can get inside and look around."

"What exactly are we looking for?" Della inquired.

"I'm not sure, but once you are inside, call me. Snoops is getting a warrant for records of Andy's accounts at Voyageur's and I hope that will answer some of my questions."

"Well, Francy. What do you think?" Della smiled at her friend.

"I've already gotten ideas on how to get inside."

"That's all I can tell you at the moment," Lainey said. "When we finish here, take me downtown to get a rental car so you will have the Tahoe."

Shep had parked beside her and was helping Jim into the wheelchair. Vera was watching the girls in the Tahoe as they got out.

They walked into the station, Shep pushing Jim. Della did her best to console the man.

"I'm sure Chief Jorgensen is doing his best to help your son."

Jim nodded. His eyes were swollen from shedding tears. Lainey pushed the buzzer and the outside door opened. They walked inside and met Officer Terry.

"Thank you for coming," he said. "Follow me, please. There is a larger area where you can wait to speak with the chief."

The officer led them past the dispatch desk and into a conference room. An oblong table with eight chairs took up much of the space. A water dispenser was in one corner, and a large white board with colored markers stood on an easel at the front of the room.

"The Chief will be with you shortly." Officer Terry nodded and shut the door as he left the room.

Shep pushed Jim closer to the table, then sat down beside him. Vera sat on his other side.

Lainey put her backpack on the table and took out her cell phone. She paced back and forth, checking her phone frequently for any notification that Sadie or Snoops had tried to reach her. Francy and Della sat across from Jim. There was a sadness in the air and no one knew what to say.

A few minutes passed before the chief came in. When he opened the door, every eye in the room focused on him. He shut the door and walked over to Jim.

"Mr. McAndrews, I'm sorry to bring you here under these circumstances. Please know that I'm doing all I can for Kevin."

The tears began flowing down Jim's cheeks again. He took the chief's hand in his and shook it. When he let go, he wiped the tears and, in a weak voice, spoke to his son's friend.

"You're a good man and have been a best friend to my boy. I know he wouldn't…" he choked up, then wiped the tears away once more. "He couldn't have killed his brother."

The chief smiled and patted him on the shoulder. He looked around the room and focused his gaze on Lainey.

"It's our protocol to question witnesses separately, so I will take you into a room across the hall one at a time. If you want to help Kevin, you are to tell me anything and everything you think might be important to this case."

Each of them nodded. Lainey watched his eyes move from person to person, a tactic to help calm fear, but also to intimidate. He wanted them to know he meant business.

"I need to advise you not to discuss the details of this case with each other while the questioning is going on."

Again, each one nodded. The chief looked once more at Jim.

"Sir, I'm sorry to put you through this. I can't let you see Kevin at the moment. He has asked that you contact Mr. Larsen's office and ask him to represent him. Are you able to do that?"

"Erik's been a friend of mine for years," Jim answered slowly. "I'll call him."

"Good. Shep, would you push his wheelchair and follow me? I'll take you to a phone where he can make that call."

"You bet. Anything for Jim."

"I'll be right back," the chief said to the others. He opened the door, and the three left the room.

Della looked at Lainey, who began pacing once again. She tried to speak, but Vera stopped her.

"Walls sometimes have eyes and ears," she cautioned.

"Mom, I'm sure that's only in the movies."

The ladies sat in silence, Lainey wearing a path back and forth across the tile floor. She waited and waited for a ping or ding or notification from her cell phone. But there was nothing.

Sven came back, taking Della across the hall first. She told him about the switched photos in her bathroom, the patch that appeared, and the hole that was left the following morning. When she handed him the baggie, he looked at it closely, but did not open it.

"Are you the only one who touched the items in the bag?" he asked her.

"I think so," she answered. "Wait, Lainey and Francy handled the framed flyer."

He took a deep breath and laid the bag on the small table in front of him.

"I'd like to get everyone's fingerprints. If we find prints, let's rule out as many as we can."

She agreed, and they stood up.

"That's all for now," the chief said as he opened the door. "Let me walk you to the evidence room. An officer will get your prints."

Lainey heard footsteps in the hallway and watched the door for Sven to enter. Instead, Shep entered alone.

"Where's Jim?" Vera asked.

"He's talking with Officer Terry. I was told to wait here."

"Was he able to reach Mr. Larsen?"

"Yes. The attorney is on his way."

At that moment, the door opened, and Sven motioned for Vera to follow him. She stood, and as if she were walking a gang plank, straightened her shoulders and looked at the chief.

"I'm ready!" she stated bravely.

The chief nodded, then cut his eyes at Shep. A slight grin appeared on his face. Shep raised his palms and shrugged.

"He won't keep her very long," Francy chuckled.

"Your mom will have him eating out of her hand in no time," Shep grinned, and to lessen the tension in the room added, "Or sing the Star Spangled Banner."

They laughed. Sure enough, it wasn't five minutes before Vera walked back into the room, smiling from ear to ear.

"That wasn't so bad," she stated as she sat down by Shep. "But this ink on my fingers better come off with soap and water!"

The chief questioned Francy, then Shep, leaving Lainey for last. She knew why. When he brought Shep back and motioned for her to follow him, she took her backpack and checked her phone once more. Sven noticed but said nothing.

Once inside the room, Lainey sat down across from the chief and waited for him to speak. He took his time, looking at her as he sat down in front of a yellow legal pad. He flipped to a clean page, leaning forward.

"First, tell me again what happened this morning. Then…" his voice was monotone, and she knew it was from years of conducting interrogations. "We will talk about the search warrant."

It was obvious he knew she was going after Andy's records. Yet, she didn't have the proof she needed to give to him.

"Oh," he commented. "There is little cell service in the building. You may wait a long time for those messages."

She rolled her eyes but said nothing about Sadie or Snoops or any messages. Instead, she told him the same story she had at the lodge. Nothing changed, nothing left out. He watched her, looking down long enough to write a few notes.

"And that's when you got to the cabin," she finished.

"Tell me about the pictures in Della's bathroom."

Lainey explained, and he nodded as she spoke. When she finished, he had a stoney look on his face.

"That's pretty much what the others told me," he said. "Now I want to know what *you* think about the incident."

She moved her shoulders a bit and rubbed the back of her neck before speaking. Should she tell him what she thought? Or wait until she had evidence in hand?

"Kevin had access to that room anytime. It makes little sense that he would wait until Della was in that room to make the switch." She told him.

He raised his eyebrows, then rubbed his chin.

"I don't understand that either," he replied.

"And…" she hesitated, wanting to make sure she worded her comment properly. "Why change out the photo? Why make a hole, patch that hole, only to open it again the next morning?"

Sven said nothing, but she could see he was deep in thought.

"The gun was Kevin's, right?" she asked.

"Yes, it's his gun."

"I figured as much. Have you seen a picture of the hole in the wall?"

"Not yet, but I'm sure you're going to show me." He winked.

Lainey picked up her cell phone and located the picture of the bathroom wall. She handed the phone to the chief. He looked at it, swiping his finger across the screen to make it bigger.

"You're thinking this hole is large enough to hold a gun." He said, handing the phone back to her.

"Aren't you?"

CHAPTER 11

There was a knock at the door and Officer Terry opened it.

"Sir, I have the preliminary gun analysis you asked for," he said. "Want me to put it on your desk?"

Sven looked at Lainey, then answered the officer. "I'll take it now."

The officer nodded, walked over to the chief and handed him a report folder. He turned and left, closing the door behind him. Lainey leaned forward, eager to look at the information. She waited for what seemed an hour before the chief finished reading the report.

"What does it show?" she asked hastily, not able to hold back any longer.

Sven stood up, holding the report in his hand. He

walked over to the door, then behind Lainey and back to his chair.

"I caution you that this is preliminary evidence. The crime lab report won't be back for a few days."

"Did you find prints? Other than Kevin's?"

He shook his head no.

Her heart sank, and she felt a wave of nausea come over her.

"They found traces of sanding dust." He sat back down in the chair.

"The hole in the wall," is all she could say.

"Maybe."

Before she could reply, the chief's radio beeped.

"What is it?" he asked.

"Someone named Clyde Bedlow is holding for you. He says it's urgent." The dispatcher said.

"Put him through to the interrogation room phone. I'll take it in here."

Lainey's eyes widened and she followed Sven over to the phone in the corner of the room. The chief picked it up on the first ring and hit the speaker button.

"Hello Clyde. Lainey is with me and you are on speakerphone."

"I apologize for the urgency of this call, but I've been trying to reach her cell phone all morning. Why the devil didn't she answer?"

"I don't have service in the police station, Snoops!"

she replied, defending herself. She looked at Sven to come to her rescue.

"She's been here much of the morning, sir."

"I see. The warrant for records should be in the courthouse next door. Lainey, get it and head over to Meade's office. You should be able to get the copies we are needing."

"I'll send an officer with her, Clyde, in case there is any opposition."

"Thanks. She may need it. Has word gotten out about Andy's death?"

"I don't think so. The papers won't run it till morning," the chief said.

"Good. Sadie called my office, Lainey. She couldn't reach you either."

"What did she say?"

"I told her you would meet her at the same park in town. Be there by 4 p.m. And Sven, keep an officer close to her, but not so close that Mrs. Watson gets scared. If my hunch is correct, she's going to run."

"Absolutely. Is there anything else?" the chief asked.

Lainey took a deep breath. "Snoops, I need to tell you something." She cut her eyes at the chief. "It may be nothing, but I've got a lead about a property that Andy owns."

Sven's mouth formed a frown, and he gave her a look that would scare Iron Man.

"Give me the address. I'll look at it. For now, you get over to Voyageurs and get those files."

"Yes, sir," she answered obediently. "I'll text the address to you as soon as I leave the station."

"Thank you, Clyde. Will be in touch." The chief hung up the receiver and glared at Lainey.

"What part of tell me everything didn't you understand? You're the most stubborn woman I've met in a long time!"

"I was going to tell you when I had proof…" she began. He stopped her before she could finish her sentence.

"Or maybe you'd tell me when it's your dead body we're picking up!"

Sven was mad. She knew better than to say anything else. He walked over to the door, opened it, and motioned for her to follow him. They walked away from the room where the others were waiting and into Terry's office.

"Chief? What can I do for you?" The officer asked cautiously. He'd seen that angry look on his boss's face many times and knew better than to poke the bear.

"Ms. Maynard needs to pick up a search warrant and head downtown. I want you to drive her, stay with her, and don't let her out of your sight!"

With that said, he stormed out of the office, not glancing at Lainey as he passed by.

The officer sat back in his chair, took a deep breath, then blew out a whistling sound.

"Wow. Whatever you did to push his buttons, you're in the doghouse now."

"Maybe," she replied trying to chuckle. "He's a little more sensitive today than usual."

"Yeah, right." The officer replied. "Let's get over to the courthouse and you can tell me what this is about."

While Lainey left the station with Officer Terry, the chief released everyone else. Shep and Vera stayed with Jim at the station until the attorney met with Kevin.

Francy and Della, sitting in the Tahoe, developed a plan to get inside The Curious Moose.

"I'll call and see if we can see the house this afternoon," Francy told her friend.

Della nodded. "The website shows it is several miles from Ranier. I'll drive while you call. Use my phone. It will go through the car speakers so we can hear everything."

Francy took the cell and dialed the number while Della left the parking lot.

"If Andy is the owner, wonder who will…" she stopped talking when she heard a female voice answer the line.

"Hello."

"Um, hello. I'm calling about The Curious Moose house? Is it available to rent?"

Francy heard muffled sounds and voices, as if

someone covered the speaker so she could not hear. Several seconds went by before the muffled sound disappeared.

"Why, yes. It is available. What dates were you thinking?"

"We need it tonight. We are close to the house. Can we come by now and see it?"

The person on the other end muffled the line once more.

"Hello? Are you still on the line?" Francy looked at Della.

"Sometimes we have poor reception," the female said, removing her hand from the speaker. "I'm very busy at the moment."

"Please, we can be at the house in a few minutes," she pretended to beg. "We are desperate for a room. What is the cost?"

There was a pause, but no muffling of sounds.

"It's five hundred dollars a night."

"We can pay cash when we see you." Francy noticed Della was grinning.

"Cash," the woman said. She paused before continuing. "I've got an appointment in one hour. If you can get here before then…and you have cash, the house is yours for the night."

"Thank you! We will be there shortly."

Francy ended the call and grinned.

"My, my. Can't wait to see what she's hiding!"

"Or *who* she's hiding," Della replied. "Something smells rotten and it's not Lutefisk, that's for sure!"

It took fifteen minutes before the Tahoe's GPS told Della to turn left onto Moose Crossing. The snow-covered road had curves and twists every few feet. Trees lined both sides, but unlike the Reindeer Lodge's lighted entrance road, Moose Crossing had none. The trees on either side made the road appear dark.

After several minutes of twisty curves, a house appeared in the distance. As they drove closer, the drab house looked vacant. Several feet of snow covered the driveway.

"I don't enjoy parking on this road, but I have no choice," Della muttered. "Someone has not plowed this driveway in weeks."

The brown front door had no porch or roof and a small light shown dimly above it. The double windows on either side of the door needed paint, badly. Della parked the car, and both ladies got out, trudging and crunching through deep snow piles. Francy knocked on the door. She had her cell phone in her hand, ready to take photos, including the mystery lady that was inside.

The ladies looked surprised when a man opened the door.

"Are you the ones renting this dump…I mean house?" he said smugly.

Della answered first. "Yes we are. I'm freezing. Can we come in?"

She shivered, hoping to fool him. It worked. He frowned, then moved aside to let them walk inside.

"I'll get the owner for you," he stated flatly. "Wait here."

He left them standing in the sparsely furnished living room as he walked into the next room. The only light in the room was a floor lamp that stood next to a worn, plaid sofa. Della hurried over and turned it on. Francy began taking pictures with her phone.

"Do you have the money?" a female voice asked as she and the man walked into the room. It was the same voice that Francy had talked to earlier.

"I'm Francy and this is Della," she said, walking toward the woman with her hand out. "I didn't catch your name?"

The couple exchanged glances. The woman didn't put out her hand but smiled curtly instead.

"I'm Maggie," she said. "And this is my husband, Larry."

"Thank you for renting the house to us," Della said. "It's perfect."

"You said you could pay cash," Maggie stated. "I need to leave for an appointment, so please pay Larry."

"Wait, can you show us around before you leave? How do we lock it up tomorrow or get the keys to you?" Francy asked.

It was obvious that the two were lying. They did not act like a happily married couple, nor did they seem like landlords. If the front room were any sign, no one had stayed at the house in a long time.

Maggie shrugged. "There's not much to see. We don't rent this out often. The kitchen is behind this room. The master bedroom is to the right of the kitchen and the spare bedroom is on the left. There is only one bathroom, and that's next to the master."

"That's fine. Where is the key?" Francy asked.

"The cash and then the key," Larry commanded.

Della dug in her purse for the money. As a teenager, she had gotten separated from her classmates while on a school field trip. She had no money to make a call or buy food. Since then, she carried a small pouch in her purse filled with several hundred-dollar bills. She called it her 'mad money.' It came in handy this afternoon.

"Here you go," she said, handing the money to Larry.

He counted it, nodded at Maggie, then turned his glance back to the ladies.

"The key is on the kitchen counter. Leave it there tomorrow. Checkout time is noon," he said.

"Thanks," Francy replied. "Is there anything else we need to know?"

Maggie gestured around the room. "Enjoy this little

piece of heaven. I'm sure you will find the master bedroom cozy." Her voice dripped sarcasm.

The couple walked to the front door. Maggie left, but Larry stopped, turning to speak to the two still standing in the front room.

"There is no food in the refrigerator. Good luck getting to a store this evening," he smirked, turned, and walked out, slamming the door behind him.

Della and Francy waited until they were sure the two had gone before they spoke.

"Did you get any pictures of those two? Della asked.

"I think I got them walking out of the kitchen. They are not good liars, that for sure." Francy commented.

"What do you make of this house? From the website, it looked much nicer."

"Let's look around and then get out of here before it gets much darker."

The two walked into the small kitchen. There was nothing on the counter, only a key shaped like a moose's head. Francy opened the fridge and rolled her eyes.

"Larry was right. It's empty and it's not cold." She looked at the temperature gage and noticed it was turned off.

Della walked over to the master bedroom, stopped and looked back at her friend.

"I can see why the refrigerator is empty. With a bedroom like this, who has time for food?"

Francy closed the fridge door and followed her into the bedroom. She blinked her eyes in amazement.

"Holy cow!" she marveled. "What is this? The Playboy mansion?"

A king-size oval bed took up most of the floor space. The red velvet canopy and drapes that hung above and off the sides had pink tassels and sparkles all over them. A deep purple velvet bedspread topped the mattress. Shiny black walls covered with mirrors in all shapes and sizes surrounded the bed. A large, round strobe light hung from the ceiling.

Della found a light switch that was covered in pink feathers. She walked over and turned the dial. Colored track lights instantly lit up, and the strobe ball spun around slowly. A kaleidoscope of colors flowed around the room, each color reflected in the mirrors on the walls.

A single night stand, initially hidden by the velvet curtains, had a glass picture frame that also glowed with color. Francy pulled out her cell and took photos. She noticed that Maggie's picture was in the frame.

"This place gives me the creeps," Della shivered. "Let's get out of here."

Francy clicked a few more photos, then turned to her friend.

"I couldn't agree with you more. Lainey will not believe this!"

They turned off the light, walked back through the

front room, and left the house. They hurried to the Tahoe, not stopping to look back. Della started the car and Francy used her phone to call Lainey.

"Hello, Lainey? You will not believe what we found."

"I can't talk at the moment. I'm still at Meade's office. I'll meet you at the lodge."

CHAPTER 12

On the drive from the courthouse to Voyageurs Financial Trust office, Lainey explained to Officer Terry why his boss was upset. The officer listened and nodded occasionally but said nothing.

"I planned to check out what rental property Andy owned and then tell the Chief. Until I knew something, I didn't want to waste his time."

"He doesn't like to be kept in the dark," the officer answered. "It's been an emotional morning for him, too."

"How long do you think he will stay mad at me?"

"That depends. If you were an officer, he'd assign you to the records room for a week until he cooled off. That is the most boring job in the department. But since you are a civilian, I'm not sure."

He pulled into the parking lot at Voyageurs, turned off the patrol car and spoke to Lainey.

"I'll go in first and let them know we have a search warrant," he said. "Anything I need to know before going inside?"

"Myrtle is the receptionist. She was defensive when I saw her yesterday."

"I see. Let me do the talking."

Lainey nodded. The two got out of the car and the officer opened up the trunk. He took out two black bags and then closed the lid. "Put any evidence in these. If you take electronics, make sure you get the charging cords."

"I will." She answered, taking the bags. "Thank you."

They walked inside the door to Meade's office. Myrtle couldn't hide the shock that appeared on her face as they approached her desk.

"Ma'am, I'm Officer Willis from the Police Department. We have a search warrant and need access to the office. Please call Mr. Meade to meet us."

If eyes fired lasers, Myrtle's would have fried Lainey to a crisp. She didn't say a word, but walked down the hall toward Orson's office, with the officer and Lainey following her.

"Orson, this officer has a search warrant," Myrtle said, standing at the doorway instead of going inside the office.

"What is this about?" He stood up and walked toward the officer. "Search warrant for what?"

"Sir, I'm Officer Willis. I believe you've met Lainey Maynard." He motioned for her to step inside the office. "We have a search warrant for this office."

The officer handed him the warrant. Orson glanced at the papers, then to the officer, then to Lainey.

"If this is about the embezzlement case, I told her I did not press any charges," he said gruffly.

"Sir, I need you and Myrtle to wait in the reception room. Please follow me now."

Officer Terry pointed to the door. Orson nodded and walked out of the office.

"Let's do what he says, Myrtle."

The two walked into the reception area. Myrtle sat behind her desk, but the officer quickly had her move.

"Please sit in the chairs in the waiting area. Touch nothing on your desk and do not answer the phone if it should ring," he told them.

Myrtle got up from her desk, gave a disgusted glance at the officer, then sat down beside Orson. She crossed her arms in frustration.

"Thank you." The officer stood in the hallway where he could see both the waiting area and the hallway to the offices.

As soon as Lainey was alone in Meade's office, she began looking through his desk drawers. She found crumpled Nestle Crunch bar wrappers, notepads, a

half-full liquor flask, and various utilities bills. He had
no file cabinets in the room. She picked up the laptop
sitting on the desk and took pictures of everything else
before leaving his office.

She walked toward Officer Terry and handed him
the laptop with the charging cord.

"I didn't find any password in Meade's office. I'm
going to look in the other office."

The officer took the laptop and nodded. She heard
him ask Orson Meade for a list of his passwords as she
walked back down the hall.

Andy's office door was closed, but not locked. She
opened the door, and a shiver ran through her. The
office looked exactly as it did on the website. Awards
sitting on the desk and the golf photo behind it. The
only difference was that Andy would never sit in front
of it again.

Lainey knew the clock was ticking. She had to meet
Sadie at 4 p.m. in the park. In the middle drawer of the
desk, she found his laptop and cord. She took it out
and sat in on the desk. Each side of the desk had one
deep drawer. She put the contents of each one into the
black bags Terry had given her.

A wet bar covered most of one wall. She opened
the glass doors above the sink and saw nothing but
wine and liquor bottles. Same in the small
refrigerator. Wine and liquor. What she found
underneath the sink made her pause. Hidden toward

the back were two gallon sized Ziplock bags. She could see a few pictures inside, a cell phone, and what appeared to be a bracelet in one bag. In the other, a broken picture frame with Sadie Watson's photo inside.

She put the two Ziplock bags with the other items in a black bag. Picking up the computer, she walked back to Officer Terry to hand off the items.

"One more room to check," Lainey said.

The officer nodded, putting Andy's computer on top of Meade's and tied the top of the black bag into a knot.

For the third time, she walked down the hall, hoping the last office had belonged to Jake. The door was open, and she walked into an employee break room.

If this was Jake's office, someone got rid of any evidence of it pretty quickly.

The room had a round folding table with four chairs around it. A dorm room sized refrigerator sat next to a water cooler. There were no filing cabins, no windows, and nothing but empty Dunkin' Donut boxes in the trash can.

Lainey took pictures of the room with her phone and walked back to meet Terry. She could hear him talking with Myrtle and Orson as she entered the waiting area.

"Mr. Meade, we are taking Myrtle's computer as

well. We will return it as soon as possible," the officer stated.

"I have invoices I must process today!" the receptionist hissed at the officer. "This is the most ridiculous thing I've ever seen!"

"Now, Myrt, you've done nothing wrong. Why don't you take the rest of the day off and we'll talk this evening," Orson said.

"I'm not leaving you here alone…with these two!"

"It's fine," he answered. "Officer Terry, can she leave?"

"We will be finished in a few minutes and she can leave when we do. But I still need her passwords."

Myrtle looked at Orson, then stood up and stomped over to her desk. She hastily wrote something on a piece of paper and handed it to the officer.

"Here."

"Thank you, Ma'am. That will save you a trip down to the station," Officer Terry replied.

She grunted and sat back down next to her boss.

"Lainey, do you have all you need?" the officer asked.

"I think so." She looked directly at Meade and then back at the officer. "I have a question for Mr. Meade."

"Haven't you done enough to disrupt our day?" Myrtle argued. "Orson's done everything you've asked!"

"Was the break room Jake's office at one time?" she questioned the man.

"It was," Meade said slowly. "Why do you ask?"

"I wondered why the rush to remodel? Jake's death was only a few weeks ago."

The man tightened his lips, shifted his weight in the chair, but did not answer. A few awkward seconds passed before Officer Terry spoke up.

"Thank you. If we need more information or need to speak with you further, we will be in touch."

He handed Lainey the black bags, picked up the laptops, and walked to the entry door. They walked to his patrol car and put the items in the back seat.

She looked back to see Myrtle watching them, her arms still crossed in protest. Lainey couldn't help herself. A huge smile appeared on her face and she waved goodbye to the lady as she got in the car.

"What time are you to meet Mrs. Watson?" the officer asked. He started the car and checked his radio. "It's after 3 p.m."

Lainey looked at her watch. The search of Orson's office took more time than she planned.

"My meeting is at 4."

"I'm going to use my camera to record your meeting. Let's go get things setup."

He pulled out of the parking lot and headed to Smokey Bear Park. It was a short distance away, and they arrived within minutes. He parked the patrol car behind the library to make sure it was out of site.

"Will you be able to record our conversation from this distance?" Lainey asked.

"I won't be able to hear, but I will have video evidence. The chief mentioned you had a pocket recorder. Did you bring it?"

"I have it and will make sure it's turned on."

Her cell phone pinged a notification that a text message had arrived. She touched the screen and a man's photo appeared. The text was from Snoops. It read "Pierce Knight."

Lainey put the phone in her left pocket and made sure the recorder was in the other pocket.

"Stand by the statue but try not to have your back to the Library building. We need to see faces, not coat backs, if possible."

She nodded. "Last time, Sadie entered the park from behind the statue. It was dark and I couldn't see any road or path."

"There is a walking trail from the woods to the park. I'll watch that area and zoom in if she's there."

"Sounds good." She walked toward the park across the street.

"Lainey," he warned, "If she is going to run, she may have someone helping her. If I see anything that looks like you are in danger, I'll be at the park in a flash."

"Thank you, Terry. I don't think she's going to run, not while she's talking with me."

"To be safe, I've called for backups. Two patrol cars are parked on the backstreets near the park if we need them."

She nodded and crossed the street, standing in front of the statue, making sure the officer could see the side of her face.

Sadie Watson was not late this time. In fact, she was a few minutes early. Walking from behind the statue again, she was wearing the shiny purple coat and matching stocking cap Lainey had seen the other night.

"Have you proved that Jake was innocent?" she blurted out before she stopped in front of Lainey.

"We have suspicions of that and are working on getting solid evidence."

"Solid evidence? I gave you that!" Sadie shouted at her.

"It takes time to analyze and piece together any evidence. Do you have anything else that might help or speed this investigation up?"

Lainey tried to buy time allowing the officer to get a as much video as possible. She thought she saw panic on the widow's face.

"More? Didn't you see the photo? That's the embezzler...that's Jake's killer!"

"Mrs. Watson, we're doing all we can as fast as we can."

"That's not fast enough. I want this solved before I leave the country..." she tried to choke back that last sentence but couldn't.

Well. Didn't mean to let that cat out of the bag, did you?

The silence was deafening. Lainey could see she was desperately trying to think of a cover for her comment.

"Oh, you're leaving the country? When?" She noticed Sadie turned her head from one side to the other, as she had done the first night they met.

"Just to Canada for a holiday shopping trip." She stumbled over the words as if she were speaking a foreign language. "That's no concern of yours."

She pretended to look mean, but Lainey could see the fear in her eyes. She pushed further, hoping Terry's camera saw the same thing.

"Canada. That's nice. How do I reach you when I have updates?"

Sadie looked around but did not answer.

"Mrs. Watson? Where are you going to be staying in Canada? I could call you at the hotel."

"I'm staying with a friend," she said hurriedly. "I've got to go. When I get back, I will check in with you. Don't bother to update me."

Sadie turned and rushed back on the path she came on. Lainey knew Terry had caught it all on camera and she had the voice recording. She walked across the street to the Library parking lot where the officer was waiting.

"Very good," he said to her. "My officers will follow her. We will alert the border patrol not to let her enter the country…if that *is* where she plans to go."

Lainey took a deep breath and relaxed her shoulders. Once the crime lab could go through Meade's computers and the items in the bags she had collected, she could fit pieces together.

The officer drove back to the police station where the chief was waiting for both of them. Shep and Vera had taken Jim back to the lodge hours ago. Della and Francy had gone back, too. Lainey realized she had no transportation…and that she had no option but to face the chief again. She prayed his rage had disappeared.

Chief Jorgensen held the door open as Terry carried in the laptops and Lainey carried the black bags.

"Hello, Chief," Terry said. "I'll take these laptops to the lab and come back for the bags."

"Fine. Have the guys start on those ASAP. Lainey set the bags down and follow me to my office. I want to speak with you."

She did what he asked and followed him to his office. Once inside, he closed the door.

"You know what chair to sit in," he said as he sat down behind the desk. "Tell me what happened when you met with Sadie Watson."

Lainey told him, mentioning to thank him for having Officer Terry record the meeting. She took the recorder out of her pocket and sat it on the desk in front of the chief.

"Do you want to listen to confirm what I told you was the truth?" she asked, knowing he was still upset.

"Not right now, but we will make a copy." His eyes never left her face.

"I haven't researched anything about the rental Andy owned."

"Clyde sent me a little information. It belonged to one of Andy's clients…" he leaned forward, resting his hands on the desk. "It appears several of Andy's clients lost the money they had invested with him."

Lainey sat forward in her chair. "Like his dad lost everything."

"We have a division of investigators who will search through Andy's computer, his bank accounts, client records, and if there is the connection we think, Voyageurs Financial Trust may be in trouble."

"How long will that take?"

"It could take several weeks or months. Especially since we can't question Andy."

Do I tell him about the picture under the sink in Andy's office?

"Sven, in one of the black bags are two Ziplock bags I found under the wet bar sink in Andy's office…" she paused, trying to gauge his reaction.

He took a breath and told her to continue.

"Since you are the one who collected the bags, tell me what you saw."

"One held a cell phone and pictures," she answered. "The other held a broken picture frame with Sadie Watson's photo inside."

"You found that in Andy's office, not Jake's office?"

"Jake's office is now a break room. There's no sign that the room ever was an office."

"You didn't open or touch anything in those bags, correct?"

She leaned back and scowled. "Of course not! I'm not green behind the ears, you know."

He raised his hands and sat back in his chair.

"Calm down, I had to ask."

"To change the subject, did you speak with Kevin? What has he said?"

Sven sighed. "Kevin said Andy sent a text message to his phone to meet at the Caribou cabin. Andy was on the floor with the gun beside him when he got there. He said he picked up the gun and realized it was his. That's when you walked in."

"Do you have his phone? Was there a text message?"

"We have his phone and the crime lab will verify all text messages and their origins."

"Are you going to release him on bail?"

The chief shook his head no. "After the fight with his brother, Kevin drove to a bar and got roaring drunk. He talked about how he hated Andy, how he wished he was dead…" Sven stopped. "People in the bar heard his threats. I can't release him yet."

He looked at his watch and stood up.

"It's been a long day for all of us," he said. A little smile appeared on this face. "I'll drive you to the lodge. I'd like to see Jim, make sure he's doing okay."

Lainey nodded and smiled. "I would appreciate that. I thought you might make me sleep in the records room!"

The chief rolled his eyes. "Officer Terry might be sleeping there for divulging privileged information!"

CHAPTER 13

S ven and Lainey walked into the lobby to find the others sitting by the fireplace munching on snacks thatShep had made.

"It's about time you got here," Francy said to Lainey. "We've got information you have to see."

"She's right," Della added excitedly. "And she has pictures to prove it!"

Lainey and Sven walked over to the table, pulling chairs up to the table. Vera was sitting by Shep and was oddly quiet.

"Where's Jim?" the Chief asked? "How's he doing?"

"He's an emotional wreck," Shep replied. "His nurse gave him a sedative, and he's resting for now."

"He's been through so much lately. Will you keep me posted on how he does?"

Shep nodded. "You bet. It helped that he could

speak with Kevin, even though it was a brief meeting."

Vera wiggled in her chair. It was obvious she wanted to say something. Francy noticed her fidgeting.

"What is it, Mom? What do you want to say?"

"Jim is such a nice man. I can't believe his son was a sex monster! It's bizarre!"

Lainey's eyes opened wide. "What are you talking about?" She looked at Sven. His eyes were also wide open and his mouth had that now familiar thin line of a smile. He spoke cautiously.

"Is this something else you failed to tell me, Ms. Maynard?"

"I do not know!" She looked at Francy and Della. "What does she mean?"

Clearing her throat, Vera answered in a defiant tone. "They told me to keep quiet." She nodded toward the ladies. "But I can't any longer. The thought that young people today turn the gift of loving someone into something so…dirty!" She raised her hand as if swatting a fly. "I'll never look at a purple bedspread the same way again!"

Sven's thin smile turned into a frown. He glanced at each one sitting around the table. Lainey knew he was gathering his thoughts before his anger got the best of him.

Shep shook his head. "I told you two not to show her the photos."

Della wrinkled up her mouth and pointed at

Francy. "Told you to put a password on your cell phone."

Vera frowned. "Password smashword. Those nasty pictures were already open when I picked up the phone."

"I'm sorry!" Francy apologized. She looked at Lainey and then at the chief. "Let me explain."

Taking out her cell phone and opening the google picture app, she handed the phone to the chief. He and Lainey scrolled through the photos while Francy told them what happened earlier at The Curious Moose.

She told them about Maggie and Larry, the owners, and how odd they acted. It was then that Lainey gasped and took the phone from Sven's hand. She swiped to enlarge one photo.

"Who are these people?" She shoved the phone at Della.

"That's the couple Francy was telling you about. Maggie and Larry," she paused. "I don't think we got their last name."

Lainey handed the phone back to Sven and reached into her pocket to pull her cell phone out.

"What's wrong? What am I supposed to be seeing?" the chief asked.

"That's not some Maggie or Larry," she said quickly, pulling up her text message from Snoops. "That's Sadie Watson and Pierce Knight!"

"Pierce Knight? The private investigator?" the chief

questioned. "How do you know?"

"Clyde texted me a photo of him earlier this afternoon." She handed her phone to him. "See."

The group was quiet, each one trying to sort the confusion in their minds. The high-pitched squeal of the chief's radio broke the silence.

"This is Jorgensen."

"Chief, this is Terry. We've found a man lying on the ground near the park. He was unconscious. The paramedics took him to the hospital."

"I'll be right there. Did he have any identification?"

"Yes, sir. Some P.I. from Florida. Last name is Knight."

Every mouth around the table fell open.

"And Chief," the officer continued, "The Canadian authorities notified us that Sadie Watson is being detained at the border per our instructions."

"Send Lt. Chassen to pick her up immediately."

"On what charges?"

"Suspicion of fraud and stolen funds will work for now. I'm heading to the hospital."

He handed Lainey's phone back to her and stood up quickly. He addressed the group around the table.

"Stay here and speak to no one about any of this case. I'm needed at the hospital."

The group nodded and Lainey stood up.

"I'm going with you," she stated instead of asking.

"Knight is a part..." the chief stopped her.

"This is a police investigation and you will be an observer, understand?"

"I understand."

The two hurried to the patrol car. The chief said nothing, but turned on the flashing lights as he started the car. Within minutes, they were walking inside the emergency room of the Rainy Lake Medical Center. Officer Terry was waiting at the nurses' station.

"What is Knight's status?" the chief questioned. "Is he conscious?"

"He drifts in and out. The initial report is that he was poisoned. Waiting on verification of that."

"What room?"

"He's in the ICU down the hall. Room 12 on the right."

Lainey followed the chief to the room. Curtains inside the sliding glass door prevented anyone from seeing in. He didn't knock but opened the door and stepped inside. A nurse taking his vital signs looked up. Seeing the police uniform, she nodded.

"Hello, Chief Jorgensen. I'll be out of your way in a moment."

Sven nodded without a reply. Once the nurse had left the room, he walked over to the bed and stood by the bedrail on the right side. Lainey stood at the end of the bed. She looked at the heart monitor and the dual IV bags that were dripping fluid into Knight's arm.

A person lying in a hospital bed rarely had a

cheerful expression on their face. She noticed that
Knight's face was tanned and his skin looked like
wrinkled leather. His thick brown hair was plastered to
his forehead, as if an entire can of mousse had been
used to keep it in place.

*He looks like an Earl Shive guy selling junk on television
for $9.95. I wouldn't trust him.*

She reached into her coat pocket and turned on her
recorder, just in case.

"Mr. Knight?" The chief said trying to wake him.
"Mr. Knight?"

The man groaned, licked his lips, and slowly opened
his eyes. The sight of a police officer standing in front
of him got his attention.

"I want an attorney." He said.

"That can be arranged. I'm Chief Jorgensen. Can
you tell me what happened?"

Knight closed his eyes, then reopened them. "I said I
want an attorney."

"Why were you at the park this evening?"

The man looked at him with a smirk on his face but
said nothing.

"You're lucky that we got to you in time," he said. "A
few more minutes and you'd be pushing up daisies in
the cemetery."

Sven waited to see if he could push Knight into
speaking. The man looked straight ahead, staring at
Lainey.

"Who is she?" he asked. "Why is she here?"

"This room isn't the Ritz, but it's better than the jail cell I have waiting for you at the station. We don't serve IV's, check your blood pressure…or have nurses. It would benefit you to talk to me now."

Knight turned his gaze to the chief. The two stared at each other for several seconds.

"You don't scare me," the man said smugly. "I'm a P.I. and have dealt with rougher police chiefs than you. I want an attorney."

Sven didn't bat an eye. "You mean you *were* a P.I."

"Are you charging me with anything?"

"We are. In fact, there is a list of charges that come to mind. Embezzlement. Fraud." He paused. "Murder."

Lainey watched as the chief skillfully put pressure on Pierce Knight. His years of experience gave him the advantage in situations like this. She didn't take her gaze off the man lying in bed. Sven's eyes didn't move, either.

Pierce grabbed the handrail, trying to pull himself up. The slight movement made him groan in pain. He put his hand on his forehead.

"Get the nurse. Can't you see I'm in pain?"

The chief didn't move or speak. He shifted his weight from one foot to the other and crossed his arms.

"I'm going to be sick," Knight grunted. "My stomach is roiling. Didn't you hear me? Get the nurse!"

"That happens when someone's been poisoned," the chief said nonchalantly.

"Poisoned?" he asked, clearly in shock.

"Oh, yes. Didn't you know? You had your stomach pumped when they brought you in. Looks like your wife tried to knock you off."

"I'm not married," he snarled.

"Sure you are, Larry. You're married to Maggie…or should I call her Sadie?"

That statement shook Knight and all the color drained from his face. Lainey looked at the chief and he gave the slightest of winks. She knew they had him.

"I'm not going down for that witch," he growled. "She's double-crossed the wrong guy."

Over the next few minutes, Pierce Knight forgot about how badly his stomach and head hurt. He sang like a partridge in a pear tree. Louis Watson hired him to follow his son's wife, Sadie, to see if she was cheating on his son, Jake. He found she was cheating with a man, Andy McAndrews, who worked at the same financial firm as Jake.

"This McAndrews fellow had money, and I thought why not try to get some of it," his voice uncaring and factual. "After all, share and share alike."

"You blackmailed him?" The chief asked.

"Not him, Sadie. She's not as innocent as she appears. When I told her I was going to tell her

husband about the affair, she cozied right up to me…
and I fell for it."

Sadie had told him that Andy got his money by
stealing from his clients. They had devised a plan to
put the blame on Jake. He would be sent to prison, they
would leave the country, and no one would be the
wiser. Everything was going as planned until she
caught Andy cheating on her.

The nurse came back in to give him a pain shot. He
was silent until she left the room.

"Sadie wanted revenge and devised a plan to get
even with him. If I helped her, we would split the
money he stole fifty-fifty."

Lainey listened, seeing the puzzle pieces in her
mind fall in place. She was glad she had switched on
her recorder.

"How did you agree to help her?" The chief
questioned.

"She told me that McAndrews had a brother that
hated him. She planned to leave clues for the brother,
proving Andy had stolen money from his father's
business. The brother would kill Andy and go to jail.
Sadie kept records of where the stolen funds were
stashed. Once the brother was jailed for his murder,
she'd give me my half."

"So you agreed to help kill Andy and make the
brother, Kevin, look guilty."

"NO!" Knight shouted. "No! She's the one who shot

him. I had nothing to do with that."

"You expect me to believe that? You've got to come up with some better excuse."

"I tell you, I didn't kill him. She gave me a master key to the lodge. I was to steal Kevin's gun and hide it in a guest room. Then she would retrieve the gun and somehow plant it at the murder scene."

Lainey spoke aloud about what she was thinking. "That's what happened to Della's bathroom wall!"

Sven cut his eyes to her, meaning for her to be quiet. She bit her lip and nodded.

"Try again, Knight. You're not much of a P.I. if you expect me to buy that story."

The pain medicine kicked in and Pierce Knight's eyes got heavy. He yawned.

"I want a plea bargain. That witch tried to kill me. I'll tell you the truth, but I want a guarantee from you."

"I'll do what I can. That's all I can promise," Sven replied. "Did you shoot Andy McAndrews?"

He shook his head no. "This morning, she had me get the gun from the guest room and meet her by the cabin, early. She texted Andy, pretended to be Kevin, saying he knew he had stolen from their dad. Then she sent a text to Kevin pretending to be Andy telling him he decided to help them keep the lodge. Both texts said to meet at Caribou Cabin."

"What happened when you met her at the cabin? Was Andy or Kevin there?"

"She met me at the reindeer barn. She took the gun and told me to wait inside until she came back. I went inside that smelly barn and closed the door. About fifteen minutes later, I heard a gunshot. I left the barn to head to the cabin. But someone was coming up the path, so I hid back inside. A few minutes later, Sadie came through the back door. We ran to where we hid her car and drove away."

"Did you go back to her apartment?"

"McAndrews had a house nearby where she would meet him. We drove there to hide."

The Curious Moose. So that's why they were there when Francy and Della called. They were waiting to make sure they arrested Kevin for Andy's murder.

Knight's voice trailed off and his eyes closed. He began snoring lightly. Sven motioned for Lainey to follow him, and they left the room. The chief called to Officer Terry, who was still standing at the nurses' station.

"We need a guard posted here. Make sure he is handcuffed and has no visitors. As soon as he is released, take him to the station and book him."

He turned to Lainey. "I need your recorder," he said, putting out his hand.

"You knew I turned it on?"

"I had a hunch you did."

She grinned and handed him the recorder. "I'd like it back when you're finished."

He nodded and handed the recorder to his officer. "Take this to the crime lab. It's got a confession on it."

"Sure thing, Chief," Terry answered. "The night shift is coming on. I'll have Martinson stand guard. By the way, we've got Sadie Watson at the station. She's not a happy camper, that's for sure. She tried to bite Chassen."

"Book her on murder charges. Use a straightjacket to restrain her if you need to."

"I think they've done that!" he chuckled. "Surprising how quickly that calms the savage beast."

"Thanks. After you drop off the recorder, go home. You've done a good day's work. I'll check in with you tomorrow."

The officer smiled and walked away.

Lainey watched the officer leave and felt a wave of exhaustion hit her. She looked at Sven. He looked a bit tired, too.

"Well, Chief, still think I'm stubborn? Am I still in the doghouse?"

"Absolutely. But right now," he looked at his wristwatch, "I'm thinking that the Dunkin' Donuts night crew has just finished baking a fresh batch. What say we make a safety check and test them out?"

Laughing, she smiled. "Sounds like you've made these safety checks before."

"Maybe a few times. Police and donuts have been known to work well together!"

CHAPTER 14

It had been a long night and Lainey's cell phone alarm jarred her awake promptly at 5 a.m. She yawned and stretched, wishing she had a mocha frappe on the nightstand for a caffeine pick-me-up. By 5:45, she walked out her room and down to the cafe. Shep would have breakfast ready and she was eager to tell them the events from last night.

The smell of griddle cakes and maple syrup filled the hallway and made her stomach growl. The blueberry donut she had eaten at Dunkin' Donuts early that morning was good, but not filling.

"Morning, Shep," she said, walking into Bella's. "Smells great this morning!"

"The girls are in the kitchen helping. We all want to know what's happening with..." he stopped speaking and ran toward the door. Kevin was pushing Jim's wheelchair into the cafe.

"Kevin!" Shep put out his hand. "So glad you're here, son!"

"Me, too, Mr. Morton. Me, too." He gave the man a big hug.

"Girls! Look what Jim dragged in this morning," Shep yelled toward the kitchen.

"It's great to see you, Kevin," Lainey smiled and walked over to hug him. "I'd hoped they would release you last night."

He smiled and nodded. "I'm still in shock."

"Oh, my gracious!" Vera exclaimed. "Kevin! I knew you were innocent! Get over here and give me a bear hug!"

He grinned and walked to meet her. She almost knocked him down when she hugged him. Francy and Della waited their turns to hug him.

"I couldn't sleep a wink worrying about you," Della said, then added. "Or maybe, Francy snores so loudly I haven't been able to sleep since having to move into her room."

"Ha! I snore? For Pete's sake, you sound like a foghorn!" she laughed. "So good to see you, Kevin."

"Everyone sit down. The cakes are ready. We can talk while we eat." Shep said.

The group gathered around a table, talking and grinning. Shep brought out two enormous platters full of griddle cakes, warmed maple syrup, and, of course, crispy bacon.

"Let's eat while it's hot," he said. "I can make more if we need."

Jim had been quiet, smiling and nodding. He watched as the group filled their plates and began eating. He looked at his son, then at each person sitting around the table. His eyes filled with tears.

"The past few days have been more than devastating to me," he began. "Preparing to lose the lodge after the years dear Peg and I spent here was hard." He stopped, wiped his tears, and cleared his throat.

"The thought of losing not one son, but both…" his voice trailed off.

Kevin put his arm around him. "You don't need to talk, Dad. We understand."

"Yes, I need to talk. I have learned that grief never goes away. As time passes, you learn to live with it and not let it control your life. Andy was my son, and a parent loves their children. I didn't like everything he did in his life…but I will always love him."

Everyone at the table nodded, their eyes misty and their hearts grieving for Jim. For a few minutes, they ate in silence. Slowly, the mood around the table lightened, and the conversation turned to readying the lodge for the rest of the Christmas guests. Jim ate a little, then put his fork down.

"Shep, this was excellent. I only wish I had a bigger

appetite." He smiled. "I hope everyone will forgive me, but I'd like to go back to my room and rest." He looked at Kevin. "Do you have time to wheel me back?"

Kevin stood up and kissed his dad on the top of his head. "You never have to ask, Dad. I will always have time for you."

The group said goodbye and watched as they left the cafe. It was quiet for a moment. Vera interrupted the silence by asking the question that everyone wanted to ask but hadn't. She looked at Lainey.

"Now, tell us what happened. Who killed Andy, and why?"

"Remember, this is a long way from being completed and many details of the case will come out over the course of the investigation." Lainey said.

"Yes, yes, we know that," Vera answered impatiently. "What happened at the hospital? Where are the people pretending to be Larry and Maggie? When did…"

"Sweetie, she can't tell us if you keep talking," Shep said. He held up his first finger to his lips. "Now don't get mad, but hush for a minute!"

She crossed her arms and grumbled. "Okay, okay."

Fighting the urge to laugh, Lainey began explaining the events of the evening before. She told them that Andy had been embezzling money from his clients, including Jim, for some time. He was having an affair with Sadie Watson. Their plan was to frame Jake, her husband, for the embezzlement and skip the country once he was convicted and in prison.

Unknown to either of them, Jake Watson's father had hired Pierce Knight. He was to find out if Sadie was cheating on Jake. Once Knight had proof of the affair with Andy, he blackmailed Sadie for half the money she and Andy had stashed away.

"But who killed Jake? Andy or Sadie?" Della asked.

Lainey shook her head slowly. "Sadie loved money and expensive things. She threatened to leave Jake many times. When he found out about the affair, it devastated him. The pressure of being accused of embezzlement combined with the thought of losing the one he loved was too much for him. He killed himself."

"That's so sad," Francy replied. "Poor man. If Jake was out of the picture, why didn't Sadie and Andy run off as they planned?"

"She caught Andy cheating with another woman and vowed to get revenge."

"What's that old saying? Hades hath no wrath like a scorned woman?" Shep raised his eyebrows and looked at Vera.

"The word is 'fury', not wrath." She corrected him, then smiled.

"Once Knight knew Jake was gone, he put his plan of blackmail into action. Sadie played a convincing part, sidling up to Knight. He fell for her hook, line, and sinker." Lainey said.

"Is that why they pretended to be married?" Shep asked. "Which one killed Andy?"

"This case is a long way from being solved," Lainey answered. "According to Knight, Sadie knew that Andy and Kevin did not get along. She also knew that Jim was one of the client accounts he had stolen money from."

"That's why Jim didn't have the money to keep the lodge!" Della stated in shock. "What a cad!"

"Sadie created an elaborate plan to kill Andy and frame Kevin," Lainey continued. "Pierce Knight agreed to help her. He claims she is the one who shot Andy."

Vera sighed deeply. "How can anyone be that cruel?" She shook her head, then stopped. "Wait...Andy was dead, and the police arrested Kevin. Why was this Knight guy in the hospital?"

"Great question, Vera. Sadie tried to poison him and keep all the money for herself. Once Knight found out, he told the entire story to Chief Jorgenson."

"He's a stoolie. A snitcher. A real rat fink!" Vera declared.

"Mom, you watch too many old crime movies. The words 'rat fink' haven't been used since the 1950's." Francy rolled her eyes and chuckled. "And it was James Cagney who said, 'You dirty rat.'"

"What does this have to do with my bathroom wall?" Della asked, changing the subject.

"According to Knight, the plan was to make it look like Kevin hid his gun after killing Andy. Sadie had not planned on us being guests at the lodge, so the hole in the wall ended up being a diversion of sorts." Lainey said.

"A real red-herring!" Vera commented. "It's like the game CLUE. I always pick the candlestick in the library with Professor Plum."

Everyone laughed, and Vera's smiled turned into a frown. "Well, it's either the Professor or Colonel Mustard."

Shep looked at the door to see Kevin returning, and Chief Jorgensen was with him.

"Did you get Jim settled?" he asked. "And good to see you, Chief."

"I did. Thank you all for being here to help him. He's going to need friends like you."

"Morning, everyone," the chief said. He looked at Lainey and nodded.

"Did you bring donuts this morning?" She asked and grinned widely. "Those blueberry ones are superb right out of the oven!"

"No. Kevin told me how good Shep's cooking is, so I'm here to eat some griddle cakes…if you have any left."

"Grab a chair," Shep said. "It will take me a minute

to have a hot stack ready for you." He got up and went into the kitchen.

"Great," he answered. He took the chair next to Vera. "And I hear, young lady, that you are the angel that keeps our cook in line."

Vera blushed and her dimples shown when she smiled. "I knew I liked you, sir!"

"Sven, tell the ladies what you told me this morning," Kevin said, sitting down across from Della.

The smile on the chief's faced turned into a frown. He rubbed his chin as if in deep thought.

"Well, ladies," he began slowly, "It appears your career as the Whoopee Merry Maids Service is in jeopardy."

He watched as the ladies looked from one to the other in confusion. Kevin motioned for him to continue.

"The station's phone lines, and my cell phone, have been ringing off the hook since the news of Andy's murder. People around here love Jim and they have volunteered to work at the lodge for free through the entire Christmas season. So your services will no longer be needed."

"Wow! What a wonderful gesture by the community!" Francy said. "That's amazing!"

"That's great," Della began. "But I was looking forward to spending the holidays at the lodge. Guess we'll be heading home then."

Kevin flashed a huge grin. "Correct me if I'm wrong, Sven, but I think a donor has stepped in to pay for the ladies to stay here until New Year's."

"That's right," he nodded. "The donor will pay the lodge if you'd like to stay through the holidays." He winked at Lainey.

"It was Snoops, wasn't it?" she said confidently.

"Perhaps. The donor asked me not to give his identity."

"And is there anything else you want to share, chief?"

"Two large companies will hold their Christmas parties and retreats at Reindeer Lodge. There were vacancies and now, the lodge is booked till after the new year."

The ladies applauded. Shep walked in with a plate of hot griddle cakes and put them in front of Sven.

"Did I hear you say they booked the lodge through the new year?" he asked.

"That's right!"

"I've got to revamp my menu and order supplies!"

"The Chief just said our help isn't needed anymore, " Vera said, obviously disappointed. "I don't think we're cooking."

"Hold on. I said the ladies cleaning services weren't needed. The lodge needs a talented chef to wow these guests so they will come back next year. And that's Shep!"

Vera stood up and hugged Sven, then Shep.

"He's a good man," she said proudly, pinching his cheek.

"I'll stay and cook as long as you need me," he said. Then, taking Vera's hand, he pressed it to his lips and kissed it. "On the condition that this gorgeous hunk of woman stays with me."

She blushed. "You do need me to keep you in line, you old goat." She squeezed his hand.

"Hm," Kevin whispered loud enough that all could hear. "I've heard Christmas brings out the passion in couples. Who knows? Maybe next year the lodge will serve as a wedding chapel?"

Preview of Murder In the Backwater

Two Months ago

Lainey Maynard had been licking stamps for more than an hour. "My tongue is so dry, it's sticking to the roof of my mouth!"

Francy dropped the ink pen she was holding and rubbed the fingers on her right hand. "You think that's bad? My hand is cramped into a permanent claw from addressing these envelopes."

"You both volunteered to help me," Della reminded them. "I told you I had some mailings to do."

"Some mailings? This is the third batch! We must be close to a thousand," Francy said.

"Twelve hundred to be exact," Della grinned.

Lainey and Francy groaned at the same time.

"I'll make a pot of coffee," Vera said. "And I've got sugar cookies fresh from the oven."

Della smiled and looked at the stacks of letters in front of her. "Why does Mirror Falls have to mail out these notices for the Governor's office? He's the Governor, for Pete's sake. I'm sure he has a budget for postage!"

"It's not some fishing weekend," Francy replied. "It's the official start of the fishing season. It's a big deal to have it in Mirror Falls."

"Paul says it brings a ton of tourists to town... and they spend money," Della said.

Francy leaned back in her chair. "It's political. Don't let anyone tell you it is anything else."

Vera brought the coffee pot to the table and poured a cup for each of the girls. "It's been that way since I can remember."

"Fishing and politics," Lainey mused. "Seems like odd bedfellows."

"Every news station in the state will have reporters here. Sarge will put all his officers on duty for that night," Francy said. "Things can get out of hand quickly."

"I remember," Vera nodded. "Doc planned on being called to the emergency room at least three times that first night."

"People get hurt fishing?" Della asked.

"Sure they do. Dad took fish hooks out of cheeks, ears, and hands. Do you know where the most injuries occur?" Francy questioned.

"In the Governor's boat," Vera stated. "Those darn politicians have a quick temper!"

Lainey shrugged her shoulders. "Grown men fighting over the size of fish they caught?"

"Oh, they're catching a lot more than fish," Francy grimaced. "You'll see."

Vera glanced at Francy and then at Lainey. "Honey, you have no idea how much trouble hosting the fishing opener is going to be. Mirror Falls might never be the same."

Goosebumps suddenly covered Lainey's arms and she felt a little nauseous.

Something's going to happen. I can feel it. Do I dare tell them?

For six months of the year, Mirror Falls transforms from a popular tourist vacation destination for boaters, campers, bikers, hikers, and baseball fans, into a deserted ghost town.

Old Man Winter's frigid winds, below zero temperatures, and mountains of snow force each resident into hibernation. The days when the grey sky gods allowed the sun to briefly peek its head out from among the dreary clouds could be counted on one hand. The past winter had been unusually long and bitter with more than 90 inches of the white stuff falling from October through late March.

Cabin Fever, as the locals called it, gripped every member of every household. Dogs, cats, and hamsters in town had it, too. The fever showed no mercy. Even houses felt its wrath.

Utility rooms and mud rooms were cluttered with piles of heavy down-filled coats, plaid woolen scarfs, hats and gloves, and well-worn snow boots covered with salt stains from the months of residue left on the roads. Scarred snow shovels and tired snowblowers stood in reverent silence by the garage doors, ready for action again on a moment's notice.

By the time April arrived, Cabin Fever had transformed the kindest, most even tempered of the locals into angry, impatient, caged animals chomping at the bit to escape the confines of their homes. Conversation at the local coffee shops revolved around one topic... the Minnesota Governor's Fishing Opener. It was the annual affair that kept hopes alive and locals from killing each other during the long winter.

"It's Cabin Fever, I tell you," Shep Morton said as he handed Vera the takeout food she'd ordered. "I'm getting sick and tired of cranky customers."

Vera frowned at his remark and nodded. "Oh, I know all about that. Doc referred to it as GBS... Grumpy Blues Syndrome."

"I bet he saw a bunch of angry and depressed patients. They're all crazy."

"A few of them thought he was Dear Abby! He'd have perfectly healthy patients come in and expect him to sit and listen to their complaints."

"Gossip central, that's what Doc's office was. Bet he had stories to tell you."

She picked up her box and turned to leave. Stopping short of the restaurant door, she turned and looked back.

"Are *you* still feuding with Charlie at the Bait Shop?"

He squinted his eyes in her direction.

"The supply committee voted to buy all the bait from him this year."

Shep set his jaw and stared out the window.

"The last food committee meeting is tonight. See you there," she grinned, opened the door, and made sure it slammed shut behind her.

"Darned old goat!" she said aloud as she got into her car. "How Sally ever put up with him is beyond me."

The Whoopee group decided to meet this week at Francy's house instead of going out to one of the regular eating spots. With only a week left before the fishing opener, each was on at least one committee and needed to spend time working on various tasks. Vera had volunteered to pick up something for dinner and the ladies were sitting at the dining room table waiting for her.

Francy looked down at her watch. "Mom said she'd be here no later than 5:30. It's already 6:15. I apologize that she's late, again."

"Wasn't she going to pick up supper from the Backwater?" Lainey asked.

"Yes, and I'll bet she and Shep are wasting time arguing about something or other."

Lainey and Della looked at each other and grinned.

"What's the story, Francy?" Della asked. "Spill the beans."

"It's a ridiculous ongoing feud that started when Shep and Charlie bowled on the same team."

"Bowling?" Lainey couldn't help smiling. "In a bowling league?"

Della rested her elbows on the table. "Paul said bowling was a *big deal* back in the day."

"It was. During the winter, bowling alleys were the only places open. All of the towns around Mirror Falls had leagues and hosted tournaments," Francy stated. "Women's leagues, men's leagues, mixed leagues... anything that could stand on two legs and manage to throw a bowling ball down the alley joined a league."

Lainey shook her head in amazement. "I've never heard of a bowling feud lasting fifty years. What did they argue over?"

Francy looked at the wrinkled tablecloth and grinned.

"Does Vera know, Francy?" Della asked.

"Dad might have told her."

Lainey caught the sly look between the two.

"All right. Tell me what happened," she demanded.

The doorbell rang and Francy got up to answer it. Vera came inside, apologizing for being late.

"Hi, girls," she stated, handing the food to Francy then taking off her shoes and coat. "I've got comfort food… meatloaf, mashed potatoes, and gravy!"

The conversation during dinner was light and revolved around the upcoming event.

"It's your first time serving on the host board, Lainey. Is it awkward having Raymond as the chairman?" Della asked.

"You don't have to answer that, sweetie," Vera quickly chimed in. "We know it's hard for you."

Lainey twisted a piece of the tablecloth in her hands. She could feel her face flush and her entire body felt like she was in a sauna. Raymond Sullivan, the handsome CEO of the Sullivan's Best Poultry empire, had unexpectedly swept her off her feet. She hadn't dared become involved with anyone since she lost her husband. They had dated for a few months and she was happy. Until the day he called to inform her it was over.

His voice had been cold and distant. His words sharp and business like. "Lainey, you're a beautiful woman and I enjoy spending time with you. But I'm not ready for a serious relationship…"

She shivered at the memory of his voice, then tried to regain her composure.

"I don't have much contact with him," she shrugged her shoulders. "He doesn't attend many of the meetings."

"In my day, men were polite and respectful. If they needed to talk with you, they came to your house - face to face." Vera stated. "None of this face calling or face texting or whatever it is now."

Chuckling, Francy replied, "Mom, cell phones hadn't been invented when you were dating. Guys had to find a pay phone to call you back then. And it's FaceTime, not face calling."

"We had a home phone. Besides, who had a quarter for a pay phone?" Vera asked. "Are you okay, Lainey? I'm sure he hurt your feelings."

"I'm fine working on the committee. Raymond Sullivan is past history."

How I wish I were over him!

A quiet minute passed before Della broke the silence.

"The registration committee let me be the lead contact."

"You mean you got the short end of the straw when it came time to pick a chairman," Francy laughed out loud.

"Anyway," Della continued, trying hard not to smile,

"I think we have five hundred entries so far. We've planned for at least twelve hundred."

"I've been studying up for the trivia contest again," Vera added. "I'm going to win that Mexico vacation package this year."

"What about Faye?" Della kidded. "Hasn't she beaten you the last several years?"

"She broke her hip in February and moved to Florida to live with her kids," Francy grimaced. "Of course you'll beat her, Mom."

"Well, you never know. She could send in an absentee ballot!"

The laughter that followed lightened the mood and Lainey was thankful for that. She didn't want to think about Raymond.

"I do have a dilemma," Della said. "Paul tells me that the opener is politically motivated. I'm having a difficult time trying to organize who is sitting in the boat with the Governor. Any ideas?"

Francy sighed. "Politically motivated is an understatement. It's all about politics... and money."

"How so?" Lainey piped in. "Money for the city, I can see. But what makes it benefit the Governor?"

"There are only two reasons to have an official fishing opener," Vera began. "The first is for local politicians to bend the Governor's ear and get special funds for their own interests. The second is a campaign photo opportunity for his re-election bid."

"Yep. All the major news stations will follow him like a hawk," Francy agreed. "It's ridiculous the amount of dollars spent protecting the Governor so news anchors can take his picture in front of a bar holding a Minnesota craft beer."

"Channel Ten kept showing a video of him sitting behind the wheel of a big ol' green John Deere tractor last year. The wind kept blowing his straw hat off!" Della laughed loudly. "He'd pick it up, try to pose, then it would fly off again."

Lainey rubbed her eyebrow and wrinkled her nose. "I thought it was to start the official fishing season in Minnesota."

"Oh, it is. But remember, we have more than 1.4 million licensed anglers in our state. Out of that, more than five hundred thousand will fish on opening day. And we have eighteen thousand miles of fishing streams and waters," Vera commented.

"You sound like a World Book Encyclopedia," Francy added, rolling her eyes.

"It's all in the trivia study guide. I told you, I'm going to win this year!"

"Back to my question, please," Della directed. "Whom should I put in the boat with the Governor? Can I put Democrats and Republicans in the same boat?"

Francy cleared her throat and sat up straight in her chair. "No! Only his party members in his boat. The opposing party is in the boat just behind him."

"Paul cautioned me to do that as well," Della answered.

Lainey thought she was joking. "Seriously? It's that important to keep them separate? It's just fishing, for Pete's sake."

Francy closed her eyes and nodded. "Fishing has nothing to do with."

"Years ago, Doc was in charge of the Governor's boat. Months prior to the opener, people took him out to lunch, bought him gifts, gave him tickets to sports games. They tried to bribe him to put them in the boat."

"How did he decide who got in?" Della asked.

"He put all the names in a bag, shook them up, and drew out six names."

"Well, I guess that's fair. Maybe I'll try that."

"Tell her the rest of the story, Mom."

Vera took a deep breath, then rolled her eyes. "The six whose names were drawn were happy. But twelve of those whose names weren't drawn, were terribly angry. They demanded to know how he made the decision and accused him of showing partiality. When he told them he drew names out of a bag, they accused him of cheating. They demanded he hold a public drawing with the news channels present."

Della shook her head in disbelief. "That's unbelievable. What did Doc do?"

"He told them to go jump in the lake, waders and all," Vera grinned.

Lainey chuckled.

"I think he later regretted his choice of words. Those twelve started a smear campaign. They spread rumors that his college internship had been falsified, that he was a drunk that was routinely seen in bars in St. Cloud, and that he had been sued for malpractice. It not only damaged his reputation, but his business suffered."

"All because Dad refused to redraw a few silly names," Francy shook her head and sighed. "It's entirely about politics."

Della's face went white. "Oh, dear. Now I know *why* they asked me to be the chairperson. I hope this doesn't do damage to Paul's reputation! What can I do?"

The group sat in silence, each one deep in thought.

"Why not let the Governor choose who he wants in the boat?" Lainey asked.

Francy rolled her eyes. "Absolutely not. He'd pick his cronies, for sure. The press would have a field day with that."

"I can see the headlines now," Vera winced. "Local Croaker's Wife Fills Governor's Boat With Hand-Picked Stink Bait."

Della shivered. "Good grief."

"Every entrant is assigned a number, correct? Well, since the purpose is to get free publicity for the

Governor, why not hold a press conference and draw numbers, like a lottery," Lainey suggested.

"Hmm…" Francy said aloud. "That might work. People love lotteries. What do you think, Della?"

"If it means keeping Paul out of the line of fire, I'm all for it. I'll let the committee know tomorrow morning."

Vera sighed, clearly debating what she was about to say. "Why not hold the event at Backwater?"

The surprised look on Francy's face was unmistakable.

"Mom, why are you promoting Shep's place?"

"The committee is buying all the bait from Charlie this year."

"You told Shep, didn't you?" Francy said angrily. "You know that just stirs up more trouble between him and Charlie."

Vera rolled her eyes and frowned. "Yes, I told him. So have your little ticket drawing at his place. That'll even things up."

"Vera!" Della groaned. "I'll try to persuade the committee."

As hard as she tried, Lainey couldn't stop grinning or chuckling.

"Don't you laugh," Vera said. "Shep's just a crusty old…"

"Della, I think Mom and Lainey need to be on hand for the drawing, don't you?" Francy winked.

"Oh, you better believe it. I'm not walking the plank alone!"

"Hmpf!" Vera grunted, crossing her arms.

Ready to join Lainey in her first adventure? Click on:
The Family Tree Murders
Read the preview below!

THE FAMILY TREE MURDERS
PREVIEW

"Brrrr… this dismal snow and sleet have to end soon, right?" Lainey thought aloud as she peered through her smudged windshield, then muttered, "Why can't wiper blades last forever?" She turned her radio from the depressing weather forecast back to the audiobook CD she had been listening to.

Lainey Maynard worked as a fraud investigator for a large insurance company and had clients in a seven-state area. She worked from home in a small bedroom she'd turned into her office. With the constantly new and improved advanced computer technology, she could do much of the research needed for a case from her ergonomic home office chair. However, she traveled by car most of the time to gather information.

After years on the road and hearing the same songs over and over, she decided to bite the bullet and buy audiobooks. Even as a child she loved the old-fashioned murder mysteries. She rarely had time these days to watch the British television mystery series she always enjoyed. At least if she had to drive for hours, listening to audiobooks helped pass the time.

Moving to Minnesota from Texas some dozen years ago, Lainey still dreaded the very long winters. Her favorite word to describe those dreary winter days was 'Yucky!'

Pulling into one of her favorite coffee shop bookstores to get a non-fat mocha frappuccino, a spinach pretzel with marinara sauce, and the books she had ordered, Lainey hurried through the checkout. She paid the cashier, bundled up her bags and headed for the store exit. The Whoopee group was meeting for dinner tonight and she still had a two-hour drive ahead of her.

Her hands were so full she had backed into the outside door to open it and bumped into a person who was trying to get in the door just as quickly.

"Oh! I am so sorry!" Lainey exclaimed as she bent down to pick up her books that were now drenched in her spilled frappuccino. She looked up to see a middle-aged man also covered in her coffee and looking not a bit pleased.

The man bristled, not offering to help her, and in a deep baritone voice grunted. "Look, sweetheart, we're all in a hurry. Why don't you be more careful, honey?"

He cleared his throat as he stepped on what was going to be her spinach pretzel.

"Sweetheart?" Lainey stood up as flames of fire were beginning to burn in her dark brown eyes. Lainey, 5' 4" tall and of slight build, was glaring upward at the very tall man in front of her. "Honey?" she repeated. She took a brief moment and purposely looked him over from head to toe. The man's appearance was that of a well-dressed, successful businessman. His salt and pepper hair was styled and looked as if it never had a strand out of place. The beige overcoat he wore with the collar turned up and a plaid scarf neatly stuffed inside, reminded Lainey of an 80's cartoon detective she had watched on television.

"You appear to be a nice, fairly handsome man that may have women with panting hearts waiting to comfort your every whim, but I don't know you from Adam," Lainey stated as politely as possible. "To you, my name is not sweetheart or honey and I apologize for bumping into you."

She picked up her things while he stood there looking at her with a bored, unamused look on his face. Her pretzel was still firmly squished under his foot. "Excuse me," she said as she stood up. "I have to be going. Here's the marinara sauce for your pretzel. Have a great day...Honey!" She stated as she tossed the sauce packet at him and walked over to her car, smiling to herself.

Lainey was on the freeway slowly making her way back to Mirror Falls when her Bluetooth signaled an incoming call. The caller ID indicated it was Francy.

"Hey, Lainey! Are you going to make it to dinner tonight?" Francy happily asked. Francine Baines, otherwise known to her friends as Francy, was one of the four ladies that had started meeting together twice a month several years ago.

"Hello, Francy! Yep! I'm doing my best to get there by 5:30. We are meeting for cards afterward, right? Do you want me to bring treats?" Lainey asked.

"Nope," Francy replied. "Mom has treats ready when we play cards at her house after supper. Remember it's the Chinese place tonight. See you soon!"

Lainey hit the end call button and focused on the boring drive ahead of her.

She enjoyed being a part of this group. At first, the four ladies met because they had something in common. They were widows. Except for Francy. Her mom, Vera, was a widow and Francy came to support her.

Over the years, the group had become much more than friends. They were family to each other!

There was Vera Abernathy had taken over the role of Mom for the group. Her husband had been a loved and respected local doctor and she had worked with him for years. Being the oldest of the four ladies, Vera had more energy and get-up-and-go than a person half her age!

Francine Baines was Vera's only daughter. Francy had worked as a police dispatcher for more than 30 years and was happily enjoying semi-retirement with her husband, Roger. In the warmer months, Tuesday evenings were reserved for rides with the Harley Motorcycle club. In the winter, Tuesday nights meant you could find Roger playing Bingo at the local VFW. Sometimes, Francy tagged along and took great joy on those rare occasions when she was the big game winner. Francy collected anything: greeting cards, statues, figurines, pictures, and jewelry. If it had a buffalo on it, she loved it.

And then there was the bubbly Della Kristiansen. In fact, it was Della that inadvertently created the name of the group. At heart, she was a genealogist and loved history, but reality was a different story. She had worked as the production manager for a soybean manufacturer for years. She retired and moved to Mirror Falls to marry the local mortician.

Growing up with five much older brothers and being the only girl in her family, she could be one tough cookie when needed. Della would pop in at the dinner meeting greeting everyone with a 'Whoop, whoop, whoop!' And so, the name Whoopee group stuck. Restaurants got to know and greet them as such. One local eatery always had a table waiting for them.

Playing cards was an absolute must after every Whoopee dinner meeting. While they visited about current life happenings, they played cards or dice games.

Arguably the most important part of the evening...treats! Nuts or cookies or bars and always something chocolate. Many times new recipes were tested on the group. And, of course, there was coffee. Lots and lots of coffee!

The talk this evening had turned to the recent fad about requesting a DNA family history.

"My gosh," Francy began, "All I see on TV are ads for DNA kits. Order this and find your heritage, or find relatives you don't know about, or get your health predictions!" She chuckled and added, "Who needs more relatives or health issues to worry about?"

Vera nodded. "We have a long history and by golly no one is going to get my DNA!" she declared.

The group laughed.

"I have some reservations about sending off anything unique about me. After all, is the world really ready for another Lainey Maynard?"

"I don't know," Della giggled. "I think it might be fun to have a twin. I want to know if they can reprogram my genes. You know, the ones that force me to eat more chocolate and pistachios!"

"Didn't you have a friend whose aunt or uncle did this DNA kit testing? Weren't they startled or mad or surprised by the results?" Vera asked, patting Francy on the shoulder.

"Come to think of it, one of my high school friends was saying something about that." Francy frowned, took her phone, clicked on her social media link, and began talking.

"In fact, I think several of her cousins or in-laws did the testing, too. If I remember correctly, the family was shocked that the test showed some of the siblings were not actually from the same parents."

"Oops! Bet that was a surprise!" Della smiled. "Nothing like learning about the skeletons in your closet! It depends on how accurate a person thinks those tests are, I guess."

"I think the health testing showed a high likelihood that family members would develop cancer. No, wait, it was a likelihood they would die from heart disease or heart attack." Francy commented and turned off her phone.

"I'm out!" Vera raised her hands. "Count up your points girls! Have time for one more hand? We have to finish these cookies and candy tonight."

While Vera shuffled the cards, Lainey put the last ginger cookie on her napkin. "Several of the adoption sites encourage adoptees to do these DNA searches. I've had emails and ads sent to me for years."

"Ever thought of doing that, Lainey?" Della asked.

"Nope. I was adopted at five days old and my

parents were the greatest gift God could have given me. They were there when I was sick, had a bad dream, at my proudest saddest moments. I have no desire to locate people who did the best possible for me at the time by giving me up for adoption," Lainey stated.

"I'm not saying DNA testing is good or bad. It's just not for me," Lainey finished as she picked up her cards.

Vera, carefully adjusted the four cards in her hand and surveyed those on the table. "Well, you never know. If you don't know your bloodline and want to find out, I guess it would be the thing to do."

"Maybe," mused Lainey. "Someone else can do this research. I'm swamped at work with my cases."

Della suddenly shouted "Dang it, Francy! You can't go out in the first round! I haven't drawn yet!"

The ladies laughed, finished off the dark chocolate covered raisins, and went home.

Lainey woke up the next morning with Powie, her cat, purring loudly while he positioned his backside directly in front of her nose. That was the sign that he was hungry, and it occurred at 4 a.m. every morning.

"Okay, let's get you some food," Lainey mumbled. She sat up, put on her snuggly socks, and looked around for her cell phone and glasses.

"Thank goodness I'm a light sleeper, Powie. But can't we change your clock to maybe 4:30 for once?" Lainey smiled as she picked up the purring black fur ball, scratched his back, and put him down at his food dish.

She turned on the TV and the coffee maker and then looked at her cell phone. "Why am I still getting all these spam emails?" She muttered out loud. "I spend more time blocking emails than writing emails!"

Lainey saw that among her regular email was one that was marked 'urgent – Francy's friend.'

The email was from a Mary Chase, a friend of Francy's that needed to meet today at 1 p.m. at Babe's House of Caffeine about some family issue. The email stated it was very important to meet as soon as possible.

Lainey replied to the email and wrote her name in the 1 pm slot on her calendar. She wondered if it was about fraud or hiring her company. Either way, she looked forward to sipping a Babe's strong mocha frappuccino — no whip of course!

Lainey arrived about fifteen minutes early for her meeting with Mary Chase. She was known for being early. It made her feel better prepared to be early.

Babe's House of Caffeine was a 1930's home that had been renovated years ago into a 70's type coffee house—complete with black lights across the ordering bar, a strobe light hanging from the ceiling beam that hadn't worked in years, and a slightly musty odor of dirty socks. The old hardwood floors creaked when you walked across them.

The place reminded Lainey of a little garage hangout she and her school friends frequented years ago. She grew up in a tiny town and one of her friend's dad had let them paint the inside walls of their storage garage with psychedelic pink, green, and yellow.

Lainey and her friends would bring a sack lunch and a coke. They usually had to move the lawnmower into the yard before putting up lawn chairs when they met. Her mom called it a hippie shack. Lainey chuckled at the memory.

She sat down at a table toward the back of the room, facing the front door. Having someone walk up behind her or sitting behind her was something unnerved her. Besides, not knowing what Mary Chase looked like, sitting where she could checkout who came in would be an advantage for her.

Her phone alarm vibrated letting her know it was 1 pm. Lainey was waiting to order coffee in case Mary wanted something. She was turning off her phone when she noticed a woman walk through the door, her expression confused and worried.

The woman hurriedly pulled off her coat and scarf, looking from table to table. Lainey waived and stood up to greet her.

"I'm Lainey Maynard. Can I help you find someone?" Lainey had learned not to mention other people by name until she was certain it was the correct person.

"Yes, I'm Mary Chase," the tall and a bit rumpled redhead replied as she shook Lainey's hand. "Thank you for meeting with me."

"Not a problem. Have a seat. Can I order you a coffee or something?" Lainey said.

Lainey ordered two coffees and waters and waited for Mary to get settled in her chair before starting a conversation.

She noticed Mary's coat was a black down-filled waist jacket with a blazing red plaid scarf. Mary straightened her blue reindeer-covered sweater before sitting down. Lainey's first impression of Mary was that she was a nice, down to earth person.

"I see you are friends with Francy," Lainey began, hoping it would allow Mary to open up.

"Yes, we went to the same high school. I think you are an investigator or something, right? I need help and hope you can help me. I can't afford an attorney." Mary finished as she nervously rolled the edge of the small napkin the coffee had been served on.

A hundred things ran through Lainey's mind. Investigator, nervous, can't afford legal fees. Her years on the job had trained her to listen and then think before responding to anything.

"Mary, I am not an attorney, nor can I give you legal advice. I'm sorry if that is why you are here," Lainey stated.

"Oh no! That's not what I mean at all!" Mary looked

up, her big green eyes a little bit misty. Mary must be in her 40's, but at the moment, she looked like a scared young girl.

"A few years ago," Mary started. "My sister, brother, and I thought it would be fun to send our DNA off to find our long, lost ancestors. Everyone was talking about how fun it was to find relatives or cousins they'd never heard about."

"We sent in our little spit samples thinking it would be fun if we turned out to be related to some famous person. It was only for fun," she stated as she stared at her coffee cup.

"I've heard of these kits, Mary, but I haven't personally had any experience with them. How do you think I can help you?"

"My brother had different results from my sister and me," Mary said flatly. "Seems he had a different mother than we did."

"Oh," Lainey said. "That must have been a shock."

"Yes. At first we figured it must be a mistake. You know, someone entered a wrong mother/father or data or something." Mary blew on her coffee and then took a big sip.

"But it was true."

Lainey was silent waiting for Mary to continue. She still couldn't picture why Mary was telling her this.

"Long story short, Lainey, as I'm sure you are

wondering how this affects our meeting," Mary said almost as if she had read Lainey's thoughts.

"I've spent a lot of time researching my brother's new family line," Mary paused, looked briefly behind her, and whispered. "I think his family is being murdered and I am afraid for him."

Lainey's mouth dropped open for a second. She leaned forward in her chair. "Murdered?" she whispered. "Why would you think they are being murdered?"

Lainey regretted the comment as soon as it popped out of her mouth. She was sure Mary saw the shock and disbelief on her face.

"You don't believe me," Mary sighed. "My brother doesn't believe me either. It's okay." She stood up to leave.

"Wait! Please don't leave. I apologize for my comment. I wasn't expecting to hear what you said."

"Please, sit down, Mary. Tell me why you think this," Lainey urged.

There was a noticeable, awkward pause as Mary sat back down. She took a minute to gather her thoughts and continued.

"Lainey, you are a researcher or investigator, aren't you?"

"Yes, we investigate insurance fraud of different types," Lainey answered.

"But you know people who have connections to

find out things, right? I'm afraid my brother is going to die, and no one will help me!" Tears began to fill her hauntingly green eyes. She was serious. Deadly serious.

Lainey sat back in her chair and took a moment before responding. "Mary, I'm still not quite sure what you want me to do. What proof do you have? Maybe you should be talking to the police."

"The police won't help. I tried to explain it to them. They said DNA research was not enough to go on."

Lainey needed more information. "Tell me the details about why you feel your brother is in danger."

Over the next thirty minutes, Mary explained that while searching this new family tree line, she found birth and death records with names and dates going back a few generations.

She'd noticed that very recently two of the known bloodline brothers had died unexpectedly. In fact, if the recorded information was correct, only her brother and one other relative remained alive.

Lainey listened while Mary spoke. Thoughts were swirling in her mind: People die, bloodlines die out. What was the origin of this new bloodline? Wealth? Blue Collar? Immigrant? What makes her think of murder?

Mary finished by telling Lainey that she'd researched sites that were used to identify bodies, DNA, and criminal activities. "I think many of these relatives died in suspicious ways."

Lainey's ears perked up. "You can access a database like that?"

"Yes."

"Wow. I had no idea people could get to that kind of information. Do you have a CD or paper files of these results? Remember," she added, "I'm not an attorney or police officer."

"I have a ton of information. Can we meet at my house where I have access to my computer?"

"You bet," Lainey replied as she opened her phone calendar.

"Oh, and Lainey, I don't want legal or police action here. Sometimes it even sounds ridiculous to me." Mary finished.

They decided to meet on the coming Saturday and Lainey entered the date into her calendar.

ABOUT THE AUTHOR

Laura Hern is an author who writes Cozy Mysteries and Romance novels.

She loves cats, charred brussel sprouts with bacon, and romantic murder mysteries!

Laura grew up in Texas and lives in Minnesota. She loves to ride motorcycles, and is an avid domino and card player. Music and traveling are her passions.

Follow me on Facebook, Amazon, and Twitter!

ALSO BY LAURA HERN

Lainey Maynard Mystery Series:

The Family Tree Murders

Murder In the BackWater

Curtain Call At Brooksey's Playhouse

And more coming soon!

Made in the USA
Coppell, TX
15 November 2023

24259946R00136